The March of the Berry Pickers

The Mysteries of Stickleback Hollow

By C.S. Woolley

A Mightier Than the Sword UK Publication

©2019

The Mysteries of Stickleback Hollow: The March of the Berry Pickers

The March of the Berry Pickers

The Mysteries of Stickleback Hollow

By C. S. Woolley

A Mightier Than the Sword UK Publication

Paperback Edition

Paperback ISBN 978-0-9951471-0-2

Hardback ISBN 978-0-9951471-1-9

ePub ISBN 978-0-9951471-2-6

Kindle ISBN 978-0-9951471-3-3

iBooks ISBN 978-0-9951471-4-0

For

Mike

For all the gin

Author's Note

Thanks for taking the time to read *The March of the Berry Pickers*, I hope you enjoy it, there is much more to come in the series if you do! This time we are back in Stickleback Hollow, but it will be a while before the Brigadier, Miss Baker, Countess Szonja and the Chief Constable return. So for a while at least, Mr Hunter will have to put up with being followed by the Baker boys. Pattinson will have to enjoy sleeping by the fire in George's study and Lady Sarah will have to soldier on as best she can as she waits for news of Grace and Millie.

For those trivia buffs out there, you may be interested to know that this particular narrative is based on a dream I had which spawned the whole of this series.

The Characters

Lady Sarah Montgomery Baird Watson-Wentworth

The heroine

Bosworth

The butler

Mrs Bosworth

The housekeeper

Cooky

The cook

Mr Alexander Hunter

A huntsman and groundskeeper of Grangeback

Pattinson

An Akita, Alexander's hunting dog

Constable Arwyn Evans

Policeman in Stickleback Hollow

Doctor Jack Hales

The doctor in Stickleback Hollow

Stanley Baker

Son of Miss Baker

Lee Baker

Son of Miss Baker

Reverend Percy Butterfield

The vicar in Stickleback Hollow

Mr Thomas Egerton

Son of Wilbraham & Elizabeth

Mrs Charlotte Egerton nee Milner

Wife of Thomas

Mr Edward Christopher Egerton

Son of Wilbraham & Elizabeth

Miss Mary Pierrepont

Fiancée of Edward

Mr Richard Hales

Son of Doctor Hales

Mr Gordon Hales

Son of Doctor Hales

Miss Jessica Hales

Sister of Doctor Hales

Miss Elizabeth Wessex

Owner of Duffleton

Mrs Ruth Cooper

Mother of Mr Daniel Cooper

Edryd Evans

A welsh gentleman, farmer and father of Arwyn and Derwyn

Derwyn Evans

A welsh gentleman, brother of Arwyn, son of Edryd

Constable Shane Owens

The new constable in Stickleback Hollow

Mr James Christian

A retired missionary

Mr Mitchell Claydon

An explorer

Miss Gunn

A retired governess

Miss Beaumont

A governess

Mr Johnathen Mullaney

A gentleman of Cheshire

Mrs Abigail Mullaney

A lady of Cheshire

Mr Luke Lumb

A gentleman of the Antipodes

Mr S. Carter

The butcher

Mr Anthony Herridge

A farmer

Mr Ross Pick

A Greengrocer

Mr Cedric Duckett

The verger

Wilson

Innkeeper

Emma Wilson

Cook at Wilson's Inn, Wife of the Innkeeper

Mr James Fletcher

A Blacksmith

Mr Kane Taylor

A gentleman from Staffordshire

Brendan Taylor

Mr Kane Taylor's Eldest Son

Neil Taylor

Mr Kane Taylor's Youngest Son

Miss Katherine DeVille

The daughter of a titled farmer

Mr Martin Ferguson

The baker

Mr Colin Nicholls

The bookseller

Mr Henry Boult

The fishmonger

Chapter 1

There is nothing so dangerous in life as low beams and small doorways. At least this was true as far as Mr Alexander Hunter was concerned.

Being a tall man was one thing in Victorian society. Being as tall as Mr Hunter was made life almost unbearable. Living in the lodge he had adapted to the low roof in his bedroom, but in almost every other building in the village of Stickleback Hollow, it was virtually impossible for the towering man to avoid banging his head.

Since the departure of the lord of the Grangeback Estate, Brigadier George Webb-Kneelingroach, the giant hunter had been staying at the manor house, which meant he now had very little reason to duck.

The hunter had never wanted to spend very much time at the main house of the estate before. He had always felt uncomfortable surrounded by the grandeur as it was all from a world that he did not belong to. It was also a world that he blamed for the death of his mother.

His mother had been the lady's maid of the brigadier's wife. The pair died in a carriage accident a few years after the death of the brigadier's daughter. Alex had thought that this had left him without any family, but he had not known the identity of his father.

The brigadier had always taken care of Mr Hunter, paid for his schooling and provided him with opportunities that the sons of servants would not ordinarily have. Yet, Mr Hunter had been miserable at school. The other boys had all been from wealthy families and knew that Alex was not their equal.

They had bullied him and treated him with such disdain that he had been only too happy to retreat to the lodge and solitude that being the apprentice to the gamekeeper at Grangeback afforded.

He had always thought that there was a chance that the old man was his father, and that this was the reason that Old Mitchell spent so much of his time teaching the young hunter.

But it had only been recently that Mr Hunter had discovered the truth of his parentage. A few months earlier, the brigadier revealed that he was Alex's father, but before the lord of Grangeback could recognise the young man as his son in the eyes of the law and society, he had been called away to India.

Alex and Doctor Hales had both taken up residence in the manor in the brigadier's absence to help protect George's ward – Lady Sarah Montgomery Baird Watson-Wentworth.

The young lady had come to live at Grangeback after her parents had died in India, leaving the young woman rich, orphaned and in grave danger. Though the danger had followed her to Grangeback, she was well protected from it far better than she would be elsewhere.

But for Mr Hunter, his duty was not just that of the son protecting the ward of his father, but that of a man protecting the woman he loved.

He had started to fall in love with Sarah the moment he had first been introduced to her, and she loved him as ardently as he loved her. Yet without the status that being recognised as his father's heir brought, Mr Hunter feared that he would repay her love for him with only ruin and misery.

This concern had only increased since he discovered that Lady Sarah was pregnant with his child. The notion of raising a family with Sarah was something that brought great joy to Alex's heart, but he couldn't shake the feeling that he was not worth the sacrifice of privilege and status that he was certain Lady Sarah would have to make.

Living under the same roof had made it much easier for the pair to spend their nights together, but until George returned, Alex wanted to prevent Sarah from being the subject of gossip. So every morning, Lady Sarah awoke to find that Alex was not in bed beside her and felt small pangs in her heart at his absence.

It was something that they both knew was necessary, but it didn't make it any easier for the pair to cope with, especially now that Sarah was pregnant.

Instead of talking about things they could do nothing about, they spent their time talking about life in the village and what roles they had to take on until the brigadier returned.

When they were in the company of the rest of the household they had to pretend to be nothing more than friends, keeping their distance from each other and having the same conversations about how Grangeback and the village should be managed.

It was frustrating for them both, especially as young men from the neighbourhood kept coming to call on Lady Sarah, not knowing her heart was already spoken for.

There were times that Mr Hunter wanted to retreat from the main house and go back to the lodge, but he knew that for now, his place was in the manor. To his mind, the high ceilings and doorways were not nearly enough compensation for the emotional pain that he had to endure.

Yet, there was one visitor to Grangeback that Alex was all too happy to receive.

It was a cool but sunny morning when Bosworth interrupted the household at breakfast. The household was much larger than normal at the moment. Not only were Mr Hunter and Dr Hales both living at the manor, but they were also joined by Edryd and Derwyn Evans – the father and brother of the village constable. Edryd was a long-time friend of the doctor and had come to Stickleback Hollow to try and mend his estranged relationship with his son.

"Excuse me, my lady, but the Reverend Butterfield is here. He wishes to speak to you all about the upcoming autumn festival," Bosworth said in his usual calm and soothing manner. The butler was seemingly unflappable in his duty, and it was often impossible to tell what the man was thinking.

"Very well, ask him to join us for breakfast. I am sure he will have eaten, but I have yet to meet a reverend that can refuse a cup of tea," Lady Sarah smiled in return.

Bosworth bowed slightly and left the room only to

reappear a few moments later with the reverend in tow.

"Good morning all, it's a beautiful day in God's own country," Reverend Butterfield said cheerfully as he sat down beside the doctor after he had poured himself a cup of tea from the teapot that was sat on the sideboard.

"What brings you on such a long walk to the manor this morning?" the doctor asked between mouthfuls of his breakfast.

"Well, as you will be aware, it is nearly time for the autumn festival, and the village will soon be full of people that have travelled from across the northern counties to come and pick berries as part of it in our fair woods," Percy began.

"So you have come to invite us to a church vestry meeting then?" Alex asked with a wry smile.

"Why, that is quite correct, Mr Hunter. Without the brigadier here to organise certain elements of it, I wondered whether the Lady Sarah, as his ward, would mind taking up those duties this year," the reverend said hopefully.

"Of course I shall do all that I can to help, reverend," Lady Sarah smiled warmly.

"Splendid, splendid, it is good to know that Grangeback and Stickleback Hollow are still in good hands.

The meeting is tonight at 7 o'clock, but please don't feel that you all must attend," the reverend said as he sipped his tea with delight.

"Don't worry, reverend, I'm sure that Edryd, Derwyn and I will have plenty to occupy us here," Alex replied with an expression that barely concealed his relief at not having to attend a church vestry meeting.

"I am glad to hear it, Mr Hunter, your snoring in the last church vestry meeting was not the most helpful addition," the reverend said sternly.

"Neither was it the most unhelpful contribution made though," the doctor laughed and dropped his fork in the process.

"Clearly your church vestry meetings are far more interesting than those at home," Edryd said with a raised eyebrow.

"What happened at the last council meeting to make the doctor laugh so?" Derwyn asked.

"Miss Jessica Hales accompanied the doctor to the meeting," the reverend began.

"She set her skirt on fire trying to chase a cat out of the room," the doctor managed to stop laughing long enough to speak, and then started laughing again. He was joined by Edryd in his laughter as he had known the doctor's sister for a long time. The thought of a woman who complained of being cold on the hottest summer days having her skirts catch on fire was an irony the Welshman couldn't help but find amusing.

"I trust that she won't be attending any future meetings?" the reverend enquired politely when the laughter had subsided.

"I am not sure she will be visiting again. She has a suitor. He's a widower, a lawyer and father of two children. She seems rather taken with the chap from her letters, and it shouldn't be too long before she is no longer Miss Hales," the doctor replied.

"Then pass on my congratulations to her. Lady Sarah, I look forward to seeing you at the church vestry meeting tonight. The rest of you, I look forward to seeing on Sunday," the reverend said as he finished his tea, stood up from the table and left for his long return walk in the glorious sunshine.

Chapter 2

Stanley and Lee Baker were not at the breakfast table that morning. Though they were in the care of the household of Grangeback whilst their mother was away with the brigadier, they rarely join Lady Sarah and her company for any meal.

They spent hours running around the grounds of the manor with Pattinson, Mr Hunter's Akita, playing games and enjoying the freedom of not running errands all day.

The boys were used to helping their mother and were often used by people around the village run important messages about. But they were both growing up quickly, and it would soon be time for them to be apprenticed to a trade.

Neither boy was suited for the tailoring work that their mother did, and she already had a young girl and a boy that would take up apprenticeships with her when her sons had jobs of their own. But Stanley and Lee were not quite ready to choose careers just yet.

When they weren't playing with Pattinson, they spent their time following Mr Hunter around the grounds of

Grangeback as he went about his duties as gamekeeper and groundskeeper.

The two boys secretly hoped that the hunter would let them become his apprentices, but neither of the boys had the courage to ask him for fear that Alex would say no.

So they played with the dog, went to Cooky for their meals and ate in the kitchen whilst Pattinson wolfed down the scraps the kitchen servants threw his way. For the two Baker boys, the few months they spent at Grangeback under the care of the household would be the best days of their lives, but that was something they would learn much later.

The two boys and the dog were already outside and playing when the reverend arrived and there were still there when he left.

"Good morning, boys," the reverend said as he passed them on his way back.

"Good morning, Reverend Butterfield," the two boys chorused between bursts of laughter.

"I see I am not the only one making the most out of such a fine day," the reverend grinned and couldn't help but feel that much happier for seeing the two boys so happy and well cared for.

Percy knew that the pair had not had the best start in life. They had been left on the doorstep by Miss Baker and taken in by the seamstress.

For those that didn't know that the pair had been abandoned, they often judged and passed loud, obnoxious comments about Miss Baker and her sons as they passed them in the street.

But at Grangeback, they were safe from the judgement of others. They were simply children at play, something that they would never have known had they been left on the steps of a workhouse instead of that of Miss Angela Baker.

The reverend made his way down the road towards the village of Stickleback Hollow. It was a day that was warm for the time of year, and the slight breeze was the only reminder that winter was not far away.

The reverend was getting on in years, and he knew all too well that he would soon be sleeping the long sleep under the ground he trod upon with such joy.

But whilst he still walked upon this earth, he was determined to make the most of each day that God had given him. Percy had a lot to do before the meeting that night, but he had time enough in the day to stop and smell the roses.

At Grangeback there had always been a rose garden, but it was on the far side of the house, which meant that very few people ever visited it, unless the member of the household they were calling on was outside in the rose garden.

However, Lady Sarah loved the flowers in that little garden so much, she had asked the gardeners to take clippings from her favourites and plant them on either side of the footpath that ran between the great house and the village.

This had delighted most of the village and the Grangeback household staff as the young lady had brought something that was once almost exclusively for the enjoyment of the family so now they were there for all to share in.

The Reverend had been particularly happy with the lady's request and had been eagerly awaiting the first blooms of the newly planted bushes. It wouldn't be until after the frosts of winter had passed, but the man of God could almost smell the sweet scent in the air as he walked.

As he reached the village he could feel an edge of excitement in the air, it was an atmosphere that seemed to descend on the village every year before the festival and promised that the people of Stickleback Hollow would do their best to make the festival even more spectacular than the last.

There were several people in the village that would be expecting a visit from the reverend before the parish meeting, but there was only one man that Percy Butterfield intended to visit.

Mr Mitchell Claydon.

Mr Claydon was a man who was surprisingly active in village life. Whenever there was a fair or event, Mr Claydon was bound to be involved in some way. It was something that had gone mostly unnoticed by the inhabitants of the village.

It wasn't because Mr Claydon was a figure that was easy to ignore, but rather he didn't make a fuss about any just reward. He saw what needed to be done and simply did it. It was something that even the Reverend Percy Butterfield had missed, that is until the brigadier was not there.

Brigadier George Webb-Kneelingroach was a man that was hard to miss at the best of times. His position as Lord of the Manor meant that he was a very well-known figure, not only in Stickleback Hollow, but high society across the whole of England. He was also a very outgoing man. Nothing was too much trouble, something that was considered unusual from one of the landed gentry in most parts of the country.

Because of this, people often overlooked how much

others contributed. Those that wanted recognition for their works soon stopped offering their help as their actions couldn't be seen in the shadow of the brigadier, but Mitchell Claydon was different.

He never wanted recognition for his work, and he was quite glad to have the brigadier's shadow to hide in. However, that had all changed when the brigadier had been called away. Mr Claydon had done what he had always done when fairs and fetes were being held, and he even took to doing some of the things that the brigadier would do at the Sunday service.

He didn't ask for thanks and even shrunk from the faint praise that the reverend had garnished the explorer with.

Percy Butterfield found it a rather strange thing that the explorer shrank from local fame when his name was so well-known in London.

Mr Claydon had made a name for himself exploring some of the most remote parts of the world. He had fascinating stories to tell, but he was a rather introverted man. Mitchell could be the life and soul at a party. He could be outgoing when it was called for, but he was much more comfortable in his own company or that of one other person – something that came from travelling so extensively to places where civilisation did not exist.

The reverend found Mr Claydon to be excellent company, and his work ethic was something that helped make event organisation much easier.

He walked down the lane that led to Mitchell's house and knocked firmly on the door.

It didn't take long for the explorer to answer the door.

"My dear reverend, come in, come in, what brings you so far from the church on this fine autumn day?" Mr Claydon beamed and boomed as he ushered the vicar into his home.

Reverend Butterfield found himself being planted in a plush armchair by the fire as Mr Claydon found some tea for him.

The explorer's house was always in a state of some disarray. There were trophies and trinkets that adorned the walls, bookshelves and stood in odd corners, but Mitchell Claydon was not a man who was really suited to housekeeping.

The reverend had often thought that the explorer needed a wife or at least a housekeeper to look after his home, but it was difficult to bring up such topics with Mr Claydon. The moment any conversation about domestic life was begun, the explorer would steer the topic towards one of his adventures.

He did this with such ease and charm that it was often half an hour before anyone realised what Mr Claydon had done if they realised at all.

Mr   Claydon was not out of the room for long, but it was long enough for the vicar to find a chair to sit on that did not have something strewn over the top of it.

The explorer came back into the room carrying a tray of mismatched china, but he brought tea from some of the furthest reaches of the Empire with him, so Reverend Butterfield was happy to ignore the lack of co-ordination in the tea set.

"I am here about the meeting this evening. I do hope you will be there," Percy said as Mitchell poured milk from a small rose-covered milk jug into a reddy brown Chinese pattern cup on a white a blue floral saucer and a lavender spring cup on a pink, blue and gold border patterned saucer.

The sugar bowl had a pink willow pattern, and the teapot had a fluted green and white leaf and brown twig design. Only the silver spoons on the side of each saucer matched each other. The cake plate had a rather thick and delicious looking plum cake on it, but it did nothing to hide the square shape ore the yellow border on the china pattern.

"Yes, yes, I have every intention of making my way there after I have been to Wilson's Inn for dinner. Emma has promised me a steak and kidney pudding this evening that I cannot refuse," Mr Claydon said as he poured the tea into each cup and then began slicing the plum cake.

The vicar took the cup that was closest to him and began to carefully stir the hot brown liquid.

"I am most pleased to hear that you will be there. Your help has been even more invaluable than usual with the absence of the brigadier," Percy sighed. He missed George Webb-Kneelingroach, as most of the village did. But it was not just George who was missed, Henry Cartwright and Miss Baker were both often talked about in wistful tones in Wilson's Inn, wondering when the pair and the lord of the Manor would be home again.

"They have business that needed attending to elsewhere, but I am sure that the warm winds of friendship will blow them home soon enough," Mr Claydon said, as though he were reading the vicar's mind.

"I do hope so, but until they are home again we must

muddle through," the vicar said as he took his first sip of the tea. The tea had a smokey taste to it that was far from unpleasant.

"Lapsang Souchong," the explorer said as he raised his own cup to his lips, "It is too strong for most of my guests, but you vicar are something of a connoisseur. I suppose you are here to ask what I   can do to help with the festival before this evening," Mr Claydon said.

"The tea is most delicious, and yes, sadly I did call on an errand of business rather than pleasure. I have just been to visit her ladyship, and she has promised her support, but I am more concerned about the costumes that Miss Baker would normally supply," the reverend sighed.

"Well, there I am sure I can help you," Mr Claydon laughed. He drained his tea and picked up a slice of plum cake and began chewing on it noisily.

The reverend spent most of the day in the company of the explorer as the two talked about the festival in great detail. When Mr Claydon was due to walk to Wilson's Inn for his evening meal of steak and kidney pudding, the reverend walked back to the church to make ready for all those that would be coming to the meeting.

He had high hopes that most of the village would be there as it was a time of great prosperity for the village, though he was glad doubted that Mr Hunter would attend. Though the groundskeeper could be relied upon to make sure that there were no poachers in the woods or traps laid that could injure those there for the festival, Mr Hunter was not a man that enjoyed public gatherings of any kind and was never a positive influence at them.

The preparations for the church vestry meeting involved heating a large pot of water over the fire so that the vicar could fill several teapots and laid out the old teacups that had been donated to the church by varying people over the years.

Some had been left to the church by elderly residents of the village with no family to pass the items onto. Some were given to the church by Mrs Webb-Kneelingroach. The rest seemed to have found their way into the cupboards of the vicar when his back was turned, but unlike the tea service that Mr Claydon employed, the sets had matching teapots, milk jugs and sugar bowls; and the cups were placed on matching saucers.

He had a cake that Emma Wilson had baked for the

occasion that was already cut into pieces so the reverend wouldn't lose time during the meeting to the inevitable arguments about how people wanted their cake sliced.

The reverend went about his work with a smile on his face and sung Praise my soul, the King of heaven under his breath as he moved about.

The song had been one that had instantly seized his imagination when his friend from Cornwall, Henry Lyte, had shown Reverend Butterfield the lyrics to an unpublished hymn. The hymn had no tune, so Percy had created his own – one that changed every time he sang it.

"In good voice this evening, reverend," Doctor Hales said as he and Lady Sarah were the first to arrive at the meeting. Mr Claydon joined them not long after, as did Cooky, Bosworth, Mrs Bosworth, Emma Wilson, Miss Beaumont, Miss Gunn, Mr Christian, Mr and Mrs Mullaney, Mr Lumb, Mr Pick, Mr Carter, Constable Evans, Mr Herridge, and Mr Duckett, the new verger.

It was a fine turn out for the church vestry meeting, and after everyone had helped themselves to tea and cake, they settled into the pews to listen to what the reverend had in store for the autumn festival.

The meeting went on far longer than the reverend intended as they discussed everything from the clearing of the forest to the costumes for the parade, the harvest display, where travellers would be permitted to stay and the stalls that would be arranged on the common.

Lady Sarah spent most of the evening listening to everyone else in the hall talking animatedly about the festival and was only called upon once or twice to see if she would be able to pay for one thing or another that the reverend had not expected would be needed.

She had been more than happy to oblige and was a little relieved that the villagers all seemed happy to plan the festival without looking to her for guidance.

Lady Sarah had been to the festival the previous year, and to the small fairs, fetes and festivals that had been held in between, but despite this, she was not overly familiar with the process of planning these events, and some of the nuances of their importance and the tradition associated with them escaped her grasp.

Because of this, her ladyship had no desire to be the centre of attention nor to lead any discussion on the festival requirements. For Lady Sarah, this was a learning experience –

something she knew that she would need for the future.

The meeting went well into the night, and the tea had gone cold in the pots before good nights were said.

Outside the church, Mr Hunter waited with Pattinson to walk Lady Sarah, Cooky, Bosworth, Mrs Bosworth, and the doctor back to Grangeback.

"There was a thick fog coming in off the lake, I thought it best to guide you back," Mr Hunter shrugged as Pattinson excitedly thumped his tale as he sat at the feet of Lady Sarah.

The rest of the villagers made their way back to Stickleback Hollow together as Mr Duckett helped the reverend to lock up the church.

"Well, Mr Duckett, how did you find your first church vestry meeting?" Percy asked as the pair walked back to the vicarage.

The fog was thick as Mr Hunter had said, and the pair made their way slowly through the graveyard.

"It was interesting, reverend. Lady Sarah was very quiet for the Lady of the Manor. I would have expected her to be far more vocal," Mr Duckett admitted.

"Ah, well, she is a lady, and she does live at the Manor, but she is the ward of the Lord of the Manor and came to help support the village whilst the lord is away," the reverend explained.

"I see, besides that, it was good to see a village so invested in making the festival a success," Mr Duckett replied.

"I think you will find that Stickleback Hollow is a rather unique place. The people here are a caring community that pulls together despite our apparent differences," Percy explained.

"My last parish was a caring community, I am sure that Stickleback Hollow will be no different. It seems to be a simple place," Mr Duckett assured the vicar with a smile.

"My dear verger, I assure you that nothing here is as simple as it first appears," the reverend said as they reached the front door of the vicarage. As he opened the door, for just a moment, Reverend Percy Butterfield stopped dead and frowned.

"What is it?" Mr Duckett asked.

"Did you not hear that?' the vicar asked.

"Hear what?" Mr Duckett asked.

"I was certain I heard a woman scream," the reverend said as he furrowed his brow even more.

Chapter 3

Constable Evans did not sleep well that night. After the church vestry meeting, he had led the group of villages back down the streets of Stickleback Hollow, ensuring that each of them was safely indoors before he went to bed.

As they had been walking back to the village, Miss Gunn had been certain that she had heard a woman scream out in the fog. No one else had heard anything and dismissed it as the fog playing tricks on the woman's mind. Yet, as Arwyn had reached the police house, a faint cry had reached his ears coming from the lake. It wasn't a scream, it was something else. Something that seemed unnatural.

As he made his way to his bed, he was glad that Mr Hunter had met Lady Sarah and the party bound for Grangeback. He would have hated to have been called out to search for missing people on such a foggy and unsettling night.

As he had tried to sleep, he had been plagued by dreams of a woman lost in the forest, swallowed up by the fog and drowned by the beings of mischief that made their home in the mist.

He had hoped for a quiet day to help ease his mind after such a turbulent night, but not long after he had stumbled out of bed and dressed, there was a knock at the door.

Arwyn sighed to himself as he dragged his feet on the way to the front door and shook his head before he opened it.

On the doorstep was stood a man that Arwyn vaguely recognised. He was dressed in a heavy cloak, and the mist swirled around his feet, a remnant from the night before that the weak autumnal sun had yet to burn away.

"Can I help you?" Arwyn asked as he rubbed his eyes.

"My name is Owens, Shane Owens, I'm the new police constable. You must be Arwyn Evans. I've been really looking forward to meeting you properly. Constable Cantello introduced us a few months ago when you were in Chester about the two missing women. He told me to tell you that he is following up on some new information," the man said brightly.

It took Arwyn a few moments to process what the young man had said. He wasn't a tall man. He had a thick crop of hair on his head, and a boyish smile that Arwyn assumed made him attractive to women. He seemed friendly enough, but after his sleepless night, Constable Evans was in no mood to reciprocate.

"Have you got a letter from police headquarters?" Arwyn asked wearily. It took Constable Owens a few moments to pull out a letter that had been hastily scrawled and folded before the ink had dried.

It was still legible, and it took Constable Evans a moment to read. It confirmed that Constable Owens was being sent to replace Constable Mitchell. Constable Mitchell had been the brother of Old Mitchell, the groundskeeper at Grangeback that had taught Mr Hunter all he knew.

The Mitchell brothers had grown up in Stickleback Hollow, though they had taken different career paths. Constable Mitchell was part of the town watch for many years before the police constabulary was formed, so it was only natural for him to be one of the first appointed policemen in the village.

Though the village was too big for one policeman on his own at Constable Mitchell's age, so not long after, Constable Evans was appointed to be his subordinate.

Finding a replacement for the old man had seemed to be something of a low priority for the Chief Inspector, how had simply been content to send out additional men when they were needed.

The regularity with which they had been needed to be dispatched in the last few years may have been the reason for the surprise appointment of Constable Owens now, but Arwyn was far from delighted to have company in his sleep-deprived state.

"You'll sleep in the spare room. When you've unpacked, I'll show you around the village," Constable Evans said curtly and led the new policeman into the room at the top of the stairs.

It had been the room that Arwyn had first slept in when he had moved into the police house. It was a cramped space that Arwyn had only been too glad to leave when Constable Mitchell had died.

Constable Owens eagerly thanked Arwyn and began to unpack the small case that he carried with him.

Arwyn grunted and went downstairs to sit in the faded armchair by the fire in the front room and closed his eyes.

His dreams were even more turbulent than they had been the night before. Just as the woman calling out to him, screaming for help, he was jolted awake by Constable Owens shaking his shoulder.

Chapter 4

Arwyn's mood did not improve as he stepped out into the weak sun of the autumn day. It was a damp morning and mist still curled in light fingers over the cobbles on the street.

Shane Owens seemed to be a charming enough individual with an easy manner, though right now, his friendly demeanour was more than Constable Evans could stand.

A broken night's sleep did not make anyone's company desirable in the view of Arwyn   Evans. The only company that the constable could tolerate in his current state of mind was that of Mr Alexander Hunter.

Mr Hunter was a good companion for the policeman. He was quiet and only seemed to speak when something was worth saying. The hunter was comfortable enough in himself to often go hours without saying a word.

Alex also knew when to hold his tongue, and when those in his company were happy enough with his presence and didn't require anything else from him.

Constable Owens did not possess these virtues, and no matter how pleasant he seemed to be, he was a man that was bubbling over with things to say.

Half of what the new constable was saying was lost on Constable Evans as they walked and he had to wait for a break in the conversation in order to point out different places around the village that Constable Owens would need to know.

There were only a handful of landmarks that the new constable needed to know on his first day. Things like Wilson's Inn, the road to Grangeback, the road to Duffleton Hall, the baker, the butcher, Miss Baker's seamstress shop, the church and the common were the only places that Constable Owens would need to remember in order to successfully navigate the village.

Knowing the village inside and out, from what each building was to knowing all the people would take months if not years for the new constable to master. But time was going by, and Constable Evans was struggling to get to the major landmarks, let alone point them out to the new constable.

A tour around the village that should have taken an hour was now into its third hour, and Arwyn was beginning to wonder who was trying to punish him when he spied Lady

Sarah and Miss Beaumont walking down the lane towards them.

Constable Evans had been avoiding introducing the new constable to anyone in the village for fear that Shane would talk even more than he was now, but Arwyn couldn't ignore Lady Sarah, and she might be able to actually help him with Constable Owens.

"Good morning, Arwyn, who is your companion?" Lady Sarah beamed when she was close enough to talk to the two men without shouting.

"Good morning, your ladyship, Miss Beaumont. May I introduce Constable Shane Owens. He is here to help me keep law and order in the village," Arwyn said as cheerfully as he could, which was to say he smiled weakly and his voice sounded somewhat hollow.

"Pleasure to meet you both," Constable Owens smiled and bowed slightly to the two women.

"Welcome to Stickleback Hollow, Constable Owens. I hope you like it here," Miss Beaumont said politely and looked at Lady Sarah with a sideways glance.

Miss Beaumont was a woman in her late thirties. She was a quiet woman, for the most part. As a governess, she spent most of her time educating children of rich families and only came home to Stickleback Hollow to stay with Miss Gunn when the children were on holiday, or her services were no longer required.

The last family that she had been employed by had two girls that had both learned all they needed to from Miss Beaumont and were now both engaged and no longer needed a governess.

Miss Beaumont had enjoyed her time with the family, but she was glad that she was back in Stickleback Hollow. It had only been a week since she had returned to the village and she had already found herself back in the rhythm of country life, and she was looking forward to the upcoming festival.

Lady Sarah was glad that Miss Beaumont was back in the village. Ever since her lady's maid, Grace Read, had gone missing with the local charwoman, Millie Roy, Lady Sarah had been in need of a replacement chaperon.

There were already rumours beginning to circulate that Lady Sarah and Mr Hunter were spending too much time alone together, and as the brigadier was not in the country to safeguard Lady Sarah's reputation, Doctor Hales had felt it was necessary for Miss Beaumont to take over Grace Read's duties whilst she was between employers.

Especially now that Lady Sarah was pregnant.

Miss Beaumont didn't know of the details of the relationship between Mr Hunter and Lady Sarah, nor was she aware that her ladyship was pregnant, but she had been all too happy to take on the role of companion to the lady of Grangeback.

"The village can be an intimidating place, to begin with, I'm told that it is not exactly the most typical of English villages. But the people here are warm and friendly. You should feel at home in no time," Lady Sarah said to the new policeman.

"Thank you, both. I must admit it is quite exciting to be sent here. There are lots of stories the other constables tell about this place, and if even half of them are true, then this is an exciting place to live and work," Constable Owens replied.

"I doubt that we can promise excitement over the next few weeks, but it will be busy, and the upcoming festival should be a wonderful and enjoyable distraction," Lady Sarah said with a wry smile.

Her ladyship was all too aware that the stories that the constable spoke of would all involve her in some capacity. For better or worse, trouble had seemed to follow her ladyship to Stickleback Hollow all the way from India.

"Where are you headed this morning?" Constable Evans asked, grateful to have some other people to talk to.

"We are bound for Mr Clayton's home. There are some details of the festival that we need to discuss," Lady Sarah replied airily.

"Then we shan't keep you," Arwyn said with a nod of his head.

"Oh, Arwyn, call at the house when you can. Mr Hunter and your brother wish to talk to you, and I am sure that your father will be glad to see you," Lady Sarah said as an afterthought as she and Miss Beaumont carried on down the lane.

"She is a true lady?" Constable Owens asked when the two women were out of earshot.

"She is," Arwyn confirmed.

Shane was staring down the street after the two women in a doe-eyed wonderment.

"What did she say about your father and brother?" he asked without looking at Arwyn.

"That is a long story. We need to finish our tour of the

village and get you back to the police house. I have to visit a few people this afternoon, and you will need to settle in," Constable Evans replied and led the way down the street without waiting to see if Constable Owens was following.

Chapter 5

Though there were things to discuss about the upcoming festival, this was not the primary reason that Lady Sarah wanted to call on Mitchell Claydon.

It was no secret that Mr Claydon was in need of the companionship of a woman, but Lady Sarah also knew that Miss Beaumont needed a good man in her life.

Miss Beaumont had been forced to work as a governess as she was not able to find a man to marry her in her youth, or to have a small fortune left to her by a distant relative that would allow her to live comfortably without having to work.

For many, the life of a governess was not an unpleasant one. There were many good families with bright children, but there were also families that were not so agreeable. There were horrible children who tortured poor governesses, and the evenings could be an extremely lonely time for them. Governesses were not part of the ordinary household staff, seen as a rank above but not a high enough rank to socialise with the family.

Lady Sarah understood the loneliness that Miss Beaumont often felt. With her parents dead and travelling to a new country to live with strangers, she had been lonely when she arrived in England, it had been her relationship with Mr Hunter that had ended Lady Sarah's loneliness.

She knew that Miss Beaumont found the explorer to be an interesting man and often hung on his every word when he was speaking. Her eyes would become brighter than normal, and she would deftly avoid making eye contact with Mr Claydon in public.

Lady Sarah didn't know whether the explorer felt the same way about Miss Beaumont, but she believed that it was worth a visit under somewhat false pretences to find out.

The day was not the nicest for riding down to the village, but Lady Sarah rode down on Black Guy and left him at Wilson's Inn before walking to Miss Gunn's home, where Miss Beaumont lived when she was in Stickleback Hollow.

Doctor Hales wanted to make some arrangements to see Miss Beaumont move to the Manor, but Miss Gunn was proving difficult to persuade on the matter.

The doctor and Edryd had both decided that whilst Miss Beaumont and Lady Sarah were visiting with Mr

Claydon, they would invite Miss Gunn to Grangeback to convince her of the merits of a new living arrangement for Miss Beaumont.

Miss Beaumont felt that is was a fool's errand, but neither the doctor nor Edryd could be dissuaded.

When hearing that the doctor and Edryd were taking part in such an unusual undertaking, Mr Hunter and Derwyn decided that is would be best if they were busy somewhere in the woods for a while.

Derwyn had been raised as a farmer, so he knew something of living off the land, but there were a whole host of things that Mr Hunter could teach him about tracking in woods. As the woods needed to be regularly inspected on the lead up to the festival, it seemed like a perfect time for the groundskeeper to teach the young Welshman what he could.

Mrs Bosworth and Cooky were busy getting the house back to rights in the brief time that most of the occupants would be absent. In truth, the house was hardly in a state of upheaval, but whilst there were five people living there, a lot more people came to call at the Manor, and there were certain tasks that had been put off until a spare moment could be found. It was these jobs that Mrs Bosworth and Cooky were endeavouring to do now.

The maids and footman were being ordered about, though the footman were really under the authority of Bosworth rather than his wife, but no one, not even Bosworth, chose to remind his wife of this fact as she sent the men scurrying about the house.

There was a rhythm of chaos to life in Stickleback Hollow, but it was one of cheerful origin.

As it was a cool day, Lady Sarah and Miss Beaumont were both in need of the fireside by the time they reached Mr Claydon's door.

The explorer had not been expecting visitors and the two ladies found themselves interrupting Mitchell pouring over a large number of maps of South America.

"Good morning, ladies," he greeted them both warmly and showed them into his living room.

The furniture was covered in large maps that were made from parchment and cloth. Some of the maps looked like they were hand-drawn, others had been printed. There were some that were new and others that were old. Some were land maps, and others were sea charts.

"Are you planning a new voyage?" Lady Sarah asked

with an inquisitive air as Mr Claydon made some space for the two ladies to sit down.

"I am indeed, there is only so much time I can spend in one place before adventure calls again," Mr Claydon beamed, and Lady Sarah couldn't help but notice that Miss Beaumont's face fell a little.

"Where are you thinking of going?" Miss Beaumont managed to keep her voice even as she spoke despite her obvious disappointment.

"I haven't quite decided yet. There are a number of places I could go, but it's a hard thing when you are going on your own. There's no one to help plan things, no one to bring ideas to an expedition. But that cannot be helped," Mitchell replied.

"When do you plan to leave?" Lady Sarah asked as Mr Claydon disappeared into the kitchen to fetch the tea.

"Not until after the autumn festival, most likely not until the spring. Winter is not the best time to start a voyage in the northern hemisphere," Mr Claydon called out. The two women could hear him clinking cups as he shuffled about the kitchen.

"Then you have some time to find an expedition

partner," Lady Sarah said brightly.

"It is a possibility, but then it does take time to find the right one. It's not easy to find someone that you want to share an adventure with," Mr Claydon replied as he carried the tea tray into the living room.

The tray was full of mismatched china, though there was no cake. Instead, there were a number of oat biscuits that Miss Gunn had baked for the explorer.

"Please, help yourselves," Mr Claydon said as he moved some more maps to let him sit down in an armchair.

"Perhaps there is a partner closer than you realise. Have you ever considered taking a woman with you?" Lady Sarah asked with a wry smile on her face.

"Oh, your ladyship, I know you're a woman of great spirit, but I couldn't take you with me on an expedition," Mr Claydon sounded flustered as he turned the lady down. Lady Sarah laughed as Miss Beaumont poured the tea.

"Not I, I am sure there are many adventures still ahead of me, but not on the path of an explorer. I was thinking of Miss Beaumont actually," Lady Sarah said directly, causing Miss Beaumont to spill the tea.

"Miss Beaumont? You have the soul of an explorer?"

Mr Claydon said with surprise.

"I have often thought I might like to go on an adventure," Miss Beaumont said slowly as she blushed. Her cheeks turned deep crimson, and she couldn't bring herself to look up at Mr Claydon.

"Is that right? What is it that makes you think you'd like to go explore the world?" Mr Claydon asked.

"I have spent so much time reading about the world, it's history and the things that others have discovered. I would like to do more than just read about the world. I would like to see it, explore it, experience it, and discover something new," Miss Beaumont spoke passionately, more passionately than Lady Sarah had ever heard her speak before.

Mr Claydon smiled with delight, and the pair began to talk animatedly about the different parts of the world that they both wanted to see. When Miss Beaumont mentioned a part of the world that Mr Claydon had already visited, he spoke of the wonders there and how he would love to show them to her.

Lady Sarah knew that her presence would not be missed and she quietly rose and slipped out of Mr Claydon's house. She felt pleased that the pair had connected so quickly. She had not even been certain that Miss Beaumont wanted to go out to explorer the world, but if she hadn't been willing to go, the pair would have been very poorly matched.

Lady Sarah made her way back down the lane and walked towards Wilson's Inn. She knew that Mr Claydon would see Miss Beaumont home safely once they had finished talking, though Lady Sarah hoped that it would take a few hours for that to happen.

As she rounded the corner of the street that led to Wilson's Inn, the lady bumped into Constable Owens.

"Constable Owens, what a surprise. Where are you going?" Lady Sarah asked.

"I was going to acquaint myself with the inn, see if I can't meet some of the people of the village and introduce myself. Where are you going? Is Miss Beaumont not with you?" Constable Owens asked.

"She and Mr Claydon are talking about going on an expedition, I thought it best to leave them to it," Lady Sarah replied, "So I thought I would go back to Grangeback and see how the doctor and Edryd have fared with Miss Gunn."

"You left Miss Beaumont and Mr Claydon alone? That doesn't seem right to me. They are not married, and it seems to me that your visit to his home had nothing to do with the festival. I think you went there to push them together. That's not proper at all," Constable Owens said darkly.

"Excuse me?" Lady Sarah couldn't quite believe what she was hearing.

"You may be a lady of title and influence, but that doesn't mean that you can meddle in other people's lives when you are bored," Constable Owens continued to chastise the young lady.

"Constable Owens, as someone that is new to the village, I wouldn't expect you to understand our way of life, or what the people here are like. Perhaps, if you thought for a moment, you wouldn't be so quick to judge my actions or motivations in a matter you know nothing about. Good day to you," Lady Sarah said tartly and strode off at a quick pace away from the constable.

Something in the back of Sarah's mind told her that he was not going to fit in around Stickleback Hollow at all.

Chapter 6

Lady Sarah arrived home at Grangeback in a foul mood. Not even the news that Miss Gunn had agreed to allow Miss Beaumont to move into Grangeback could lift her blackened spirits.

Over dinner, Mr Hunter was able to get Lady Sarah to laugh a little, but the cause of her temper was not revealed until the following morning when Constable Evans brought Constable Owens to the house.

When Bosworth came to announce the two policemen, Lady Sarah instructed him to send Constable Owens away as he was not welcome in her home.

This led to a number of questions about what the constable had done from those who were living in the house, but Constable Evans was clearly relieved to have some time away from the new constable.

The visit was brief, but a pleasant one. The rift that had once existed between the members of the Evans family seemed to have been healed by their time in close proximity in the village.

Miss Beaumont was brought to the house later that day by Mr Claydon, and the explorer took the opportunity to discuss the plans for the festival with the doctor, Edryd, Mr Hunter and Derwyn.

Preparations in the village were going well. The festival was something that many had been preparing for for weeks, so it was no surprise that things were coming together well. The Reverend Butterfield was visiting people on a daily basis, making sure that everything was in place, and Mr Claydon found reasons to visit Grangeback every day, something that Lady Sarah knew had more to do with Miss Beaumont than festival preparations.

Three days before the festival was due to begin, the Dean of Chester Cathedral came to the village. George Davys, the Dean of Chester that had met Constable Evans, Lady Sarah and Mr Hunter during their first mystery investigation in Chester had been made the Bishop of Peterborough in May, so a new dean had been appointed. His name was Frederick Anson.

His family was well connected, and he was reported to be an amiable man. When he had been installed as dean, the

Reverend Percy Butterfield had gone to Chester to welcome him. When the reverend had returned to Stickleback Hollow, he had nothing but nice things to say about the new dean, though it was clear that he would miss the old one.

Frederick Anson had wanted to come and see the preparations for the festival much earlier, but adapting to his duties and the people of Chester had prevented his appearance.

"Things are taking shape well," Mr Anson said as he and the reverend walked around the village.

"We will be ready for the arrival of all the people for the festival by tomorrow. It seems that people are arriving earlier and earlier for the festival every year," Percy explained.

"Celebrations are often a much-needed rest for the soul. People work hard and are in need of rest and relaxation in ever greater measures. This festival is a wonderful way for people from all over the northern lands to take time away from their work and escape from the cities," the dean smiled.

"Then it is even more important that we put on a good festival," the reverend said firmly.

"I have asked my darling, Mary Anne, if she can keep the hounds at bay for a few days. If you are amenable to having an extra pair of hands, I am at your disposal," the dean smiled.

"What a wonderful offer, I couldn't impose on you though," Percy replied in astonishment.

"Nonsense, it's not an imposition when it's an offer. If you can find a bed for me, I am more than happy to help however I can," Frederick said as he patted the reverend on the back.

"I am afraid I cannot offer you a bed at the rectory with Mr Duckett and I, but I am sure that Lady Sarah would be more than happy to offer you a bed for however long you decide to stay," Percy said brightly and led the dean away from the village and towards the great house of Grangeback.

Mr Hunter was coming down the road towards the pair, but as soon as he saw people coming towards him, Alex ducked off the road and made his way through the trees and down to the village.

Mr Hunter's mind was too full to be able to face an exchange of pleasantries with the vicar and his companion on the road.

The groundskeeper had slipped out of the house to avoid the chaos that the festival had created. Even Derwyn had been dragged into creating games for the children to play during the festivities.

Some time away from the house and all the excitement was something that the hunter needed as there was a lot that he had to think about. Every day for the last week, he had been finding excuses to slip away so that he could sit in Wilson's Inn for a few hours to try and make sense out of it all.

He was struggling with what he should do as he didn't know when Brigadier George Webb-Kneelingroach would be back from his time abroad. If he waited until the brigadier returned to recognise Alex as his son and heir, then Lady Sarah may have already given birth to their child and find herself shamed and cast out of society.

However, if he married her before he was recognised as the brigadier's heir, she would be shamed for marrying a commoner. Even if he was recognised as George's heir after they were married, most of those in high society would always believe that the only reason that Alex was named as the brigadier's son was to save the Lady Sarah from disgrace. She would never be included within the society that she was born into, and her child would be excluded from that world as well.

He felt like he was stuck between a rock and a hard

place. He had no one that he could confide in, no one that he could talk to about how he was feeling or ask advice about what he should do.

All he could do is sit and think about what had happened and the impossible choice that was before him. He came to Wilson's Inn and sat at the bar, he nursed a glass of beer for hours before he threw it back and headed back to the manor.

With so many people in the village focused on the festival, only Wilson noticed that there was something wrong with Mr Hunter, and although the innkeeper didn't know what was wrong, he was inclined to give Mr Hunter a sympathetic smile each time he came through the door.

Chapter 7

"Has anyone seen Mr Hunter?" Lady Sarah asked with a frown. She had noticed his absence each evening, but he had been in such a dower mood over the past few days, the lady hadn't wanted to pry into where he was going.

"No, your ladyship, but I am sure he will be back soon," the doctor said warmly.

The doctor, Lady Sarah, Edryd, Derwyn, Miss Beaumont, Frederick Anson, Mr Claydon, and the Reverend Butterfield were all sat in the drawing-room as the evening sun cast long shadows through the tall windows.

Mrs Bosworth was moving about the room with plates of cakes and biscuits whilst Bosworth the butler was attending to the tea.

It was a pleasant evening, and Cooky was in her element, creating afternoon pastries as well as organising her assistants into starting the preparations for dinner.

The household of Grangeback was one that was always happiest when there were guests staying there. With the doctor, Edryd, Derwyn, Mr Hunter. Lee Baker, Stanley Baker, and now the Dean of Chester in residence along with Lady Sarah, it was enough to bring smiles to everyone's faces – especially when they knew there were more guests yet to come.

With so many people coming from across the north of England for the festival, the families of the great houses that were coming needed places to stay. Some would be staying with Miss Elizabeth Wessex at Duffleton Hall, others would be staying with the Egerton family at Tatton Park. There were other great houses that were in the area, but they were deemed too far for those who wanted to enjoy everything that the festival had to offer.

For those of title and high birth who could not find space at one of the great houses, there were the hotels of Chester that could be called upon to provide beds for them. This, however, was not a fashionable option for most for no other reason than the society that was enjoyed in the three great houses.

After the festivities of the day and night had exhausted the guests of Grangeback. Duffleton Hall and Tatton Park, there were the soirées and suppers held in each house that were only open to those who were staying there. Each year the three houses competed for the best reputation of hospitality, something that Mrs Bosworth, Cooky and Bosworth the Butler took as seriously as the Brigadier did.

In the absence of their master, the household were determined to finish the festival with their heads held high and their reputation as the best house with the warmest fires and most succulent feasts that the neighbourhood had to offer.

Edryd and Derwyn had found the flurry of activity in the house a rather mystifying display, and were even more perplexed as to why the festival was so important to the village.

"With so many of you here now, perhaps one of you could tell us why this festival is so important?" Edryd asked with his natural lyrical welsh lit.

"It's a celebration of a good harvest!" Mrs Bosworth exclaimed as she almost dropped the plate of biscuits she was carrying. It hadn't occurred to the housekeeper that neither the doctor nor Constable Evans would have not mentioned to Edryd and Derwyn Evans why the festival was so important.

"Come, come, Mrs Bosworth, it is much more than a simple celebration, is it not? Hmm, perhaps we assembled are not the best ones to explain it's importance though. With your ladyship's permission, could we call upon Cooky to tell the tale of how this all came to be?" the reverend asked as he rose to his feet. Lady Sarah nodded her consent with a smile, and the vicar disappeared off to the kitchen to fetch Cooky to the drawing-room.

It took only a few moments for the plump cook to be brought from her duties, but she looked a little flustered and clearly wished to return to her cooking as soon as she could.

"The reverend tells me you want to hear the story about how the festival started. Well, I daresay that some others here could have told you, but I'm here now. When I was just a little girl, there was a bad drought. None of the farms could get enough water, and most of the crops failed. It was a terrible year for a lot of families. People were close to starving and barely had enough water to get by. The price of food was being driven up by the lack of it, and even folks as rich as the brigadier and Lady Sarah were struggling to put food on their tables.

"The manor didn't belong to the Kneelingroach family back then, it was in the hands of a family called Williamson. Some said they had Welsh roots, but that didn't matter to those around these parts. Mr Williamson was a good landlord, and though he and his could barely afford to buy food, he didn't charge the tenants on his farms any rent that year. He knew that they needed to eat and survive more than he needed more coin in his pocket.

"His son, Jamie, he was a bonnie boy, and a good friend to all the children in the village, he decided to lead all the children on an expedition to find more food and save the village. The woods were a lot wilder back in those days, we didn't have anyone like Mr Hunter to keep them under control. I don't think that many people had really dared to go too far into the thicker parts of the woods in those days, especially with the legend of the Edge hanging over them.

"There were a few that had found some deer and some boar and managed to bring them back home again, but most people would just get lost in the trees, and it would take bring dogs with the town watch to find them and bring them home. I'm not really sure why we all agreed to go with Jamie, but we did. Every child in the village signed up to his expedition.

"We all snuck out, early in the morning, before any of the adults were awake. We agreed to meet outside the inn and go to the woods from there. We hadn't got any food or water with us, but we did have a few baskets and some farming tools that we'd been able to steal. Bosworth and Mrs Bosworth were both there, though she was Miss Guptil and I was Miss Ferguson. Mr Cook hadn't come to these parts yet, God rest his soul.

"So into the woods we went, full of whatever it is and vinegar. We came across some rabbits, but we scared them off before we got close enough to catch them. We spent hours walking through the woods until we found ourselves in a part we didn't recognise. The lake wasn't more than a pond back in those days, and it didn't have all the fish in it that it does now, but we stumbled out of a thick patch of bracken and found ourselves in this marshy area next to the pond.

"There were bushes and bushes all over the place that were covered with blackberries and blackcurrants. On the ground, there were more strawberry plants than I thought I'd ever live to see, and there were rows and rows of raspberry stalks waving in the wind. It was like we'd stumbled across our own secret food stash. None of us could believe what we had found. We began to grab handfuls of berries off the bushes and cram them into our mouths. Some of the berries had a little more protein in than we were expecting, but for hungry children, it was a blessing to find so many of them.

"Once we'd covered our faces and hands with sticky juices and filled our bellies with so many berries we began to feel sick, Jamie set about organising us to harvest as many berries as we could and put them into the baskets. We were careful not to pull up the plants so they'd grow back again. Once we cleared out the grove we were in, we split up into two groups and moved around the pond in opposite directions. We found that all around the pond, there were more and more berries. So many berries that soon Mrs Bosworth and I had to take off our aprons so that more berries could be piled into them.

"We made our way all around the pond, but by that time, it was getting dark, and no one had any idea on how we were going to get back to the village. Jamie tried to lead the way, but then he started to cry out in pain. Someone had left traps out in the woods for animals, and Jamie had caught his leg in a horrible metal trap. We were all glad it was dark because none of us wanted to see any blood.

"The boys tried to open the trap to get his leg out, but it was so stiff they couldn't move it. We didn't know what to do, and we couldn't send anyone for help as we didn't know which was help was. Bosworth made a fire in the middle of a circle of rocks to keep us all warm, but we were miserable. We had been so clever and saved the village from starving, but now Jamie was hurt, and we couldn't get home.

"It felt like we were waiting for days in those woods, but the town watch had been sent out to find us after lunch, and it wasn't too long after Jamie got stuck in the trap that they found us. They managed to free Jamie's leg, but he was unconscious now, and they had to rush him back to the village. The rest of us carried our berry-filled baskets and aprons back to the village with the town watch that had stayed behind to take us home.

"It was a good job that they had those dogs as not even the men knew their way through the thicker woods. When we got back to the village, everyone was waiting on the common. They'd seen Jamie being carried back and were all worried about what had happened in the woods. The moment we came out of the trees, all of the adults started to cry and shout, and it took the blacksmith to quiet everyone down long enough for us to tell them what we'd found.

"All the anger at us going off on our own disappeared when they saw all the berries we'd found. All of the berries were counted up and split between every house in the village. It was enough to keep us all from starving that year. Most of the berries were made into jams so that they would last a long time, and the adults organised proper foraging parties to go out into the woods to find even more food," Cooky explained.

"What happened to Jamie?" Derwyn asked.

"He lost his leg that night. The doctor did what he could for him, but even after he cut off the bad part, it still got infected. He was sick for weeks, but he managed to hold on for Christmas. He died on New Years' Day, but he saved the village. Mr Williamson was never the same after that. His wife died two years later, and when he died, the Kneelingroach family bought the manor. But if it was not for Jamie, we'd have all died that year. Word soon spread of what had happened in the village, and the next year, people came from Chester and nearby villages to pick berries from the woods. The next year more people came from further afield. There wasn't a drought, but people wanted to see the setting for the story they had heard. More people came back each time, so every year we celebrate a good harvest with a great festival and people come from all over to pick the berries that kept us from starving here," Cooky finished.

"It's understandable why you all take such pride in this festival," Edryd said warmly. The dean looked down at his hands and said a quick prayer of thanks that he had not had to lose any of his sons in such a horrible fashion.

Lady Sarah absently stroked her belly and wondered about how her life was about to change because of the baby that was growing inside her.

The sombre mood the story had caused to descend on the room was shattered as Lee, and Stanley Baker burst into the room, breathing hard.

"They're here! The first pickers are here!" they cried. The room exploded into a flurry of movement, only the dean, Edryd and Derwyn remained where they were, staring in wonder at those who now scurried manically around them.

"I see there are some significant elements of this festival that the story doesn't cover," the dean said wryly.

Chapter 8

With all the activity in the house, Derwyn was sent to try and find Mr Hunter, whilst the dean was summoned to help the reverend make his final preparations. Edryd was at something of a loose end and decided that rather than being underfoot, he would go visit Arwyn in the village.

The walk down to Stickleback Hollow was a welcome moment of peace from the chaos that had now enveloped Grangeback. Edryd whistled to himself as he walked and kicked errant stones off the path and into the grass where they belonged.

It had been a while since Edryd had taken a walk by himself. When he was in Wales on his farm, he often would go out to walk the fields on his own and check on how things were. It gave him time to himself and time to think, something that he had not had much of since coming to visit Stickleback Hollow.

He knew that at some point soon he would have to take Derwyn home to Wales again, but until then he needed to make more time for walks.

When he reached the police house, his heart sank a little, the walk had been enjoyable, but not nearly long enough. He sighed and shook his head, trying to remind himself that the purpose of his walk was to visit his son, not to stretch his legs too much.

He walked up to the front door and knocked on the door. It took a few moments, but the door was soon opened, and Constable Owens stood in the doorway.

"Can I help you?" the new constable asked.

"I'm looking for Constable Evans, is he here?" Edryd asked brightly.

"No, he isn't. Are you here on police business?" Shane asked.

"No, I just came to visit Arwyn. May I come in and wait?" Edryd replied. He wasn't sure why, but he was beginning to feel very uncomfortable.

"No, there is no entry into the police house except on police business," Constable Owens said and then shut the door in Edryd's face.

Edryd frowned as he stood on the doorstep, unsure as to what had just happened. His mind raced for reasons why the new constable had spoken to him in that way. He thought it might be because he was Welsh, or that he was uncomfortable having people in the police house until he was settled in and knew the village. Either way, he couldn't shake the feeling that Constable Owens had been incredibly rude to him.

Rather than give up and make his way back to the manor house, Edryd decided that he would go and take a tour around the village and try to stretch his legs a little more with the added bonus that he might find Arwyn.

Edryd moved off down the lane. As he walked through Stickleback Hollow, he saw people moving about in a frenzied fashion. The Welshman smiled to himself as he watched the flurry of activity. There were a few people walking down the main road towards the inn that were clearly the arrivals that Stanley and Lee Baker had come to warn those at Grangeback about.

Edryd wondered if the pair hadn't run through the village ahead of the visitors, shouting about their arrival to the whole of Stickleback Hollow.

He reached the common and looked around at the stalls that were set up and now being hurriedly stocked, and in the middle of all the chaos was Arwyn.

"Son!" Edryd called out and beckoned for Constable Evans to join him outside of the ring of stalls. The policeman walked over, making sure that everything was going smoothly as he passed each stall.

"What brings you down from the manor?" Arwyn asked as he reached out and shook his father's hand.

"Stanley and Lee Baker came running in with news that the first pickers had arrived. So much activity erupted, and I was just underfoot. I thought it best to come down to the village and seek you out," Edryd explained.

"Did you visit the police house first?" Arwyn frowned.

"Yes, I asked the new constable if I could wait for you inside, but he wouldn't let me in. He seemed adamant that I could only go in if I needed the police," Edryd sighed.

"He is a little overzealous," Arwyn said slowly, "I'm sure he'll calm down soon enough though. He's just getting used to the village. He doesn't know how things are done around here yet."

"I hope you are right. He seems to have already upset Lady Sarah, and I can't imagine that many people here will take kindly to such a rigid attitude," Edryd replied.

"No, but I wasn't all that different when I first came here. It takes some getting used to, this place," Arwyn smiled to himself as he looked over the people as they hurried about the common.

"I'm glad you've found happiness here. I know that we didn't do well as father and son when you were younger, but I really did want what was best for you. It seems that this is where you belong though, and I wouldn't want to take you away from it now," Edryd placed his hand on his son's shoulder and squeezed it gently.

"I am happy here, dad, and if ever I find myself unhappy, I'll come back to Wales," Arwyn grinned.

"You'll always be welcome, my boy," Edryd smiled back. Arwyn seemed poised to say something else, but before he could a scream split the night. Everyone on the common froze where they stood and then turned, trying to find the source of the screaming.

A woman was running down the road screaming, her face was drained of all colour and terror haunted her eyes.

"What is it?" Arwyn asked as he blocked the woman's path and took her trembling form into his arms.

"There was a witch in the woods. She wanted to take

my soul," the woman sobbed.

Edryd looked at Arwyn with concern, and the residents of the common all started talking to each other in hushed tones.

"Come with me to the inn. We'll get you something medicinal to drink, and you can tell me everything you saw," Arwyn said gently as he half walked, half carried, the woman towards Wilson's Inn. His father walked beside him with a grim look on his face.

A witch in the woods? Just what we need. Arwyn thought.

Chapter 9

The news of a witch lurking the woods was not something that was taken lightly. Before Arwyn, Edryd and the woman had reached the inn, news of the sighting had already circulated around it.

Mr Hunter was still sat at the bar when the trio entered and sat down at a nearby table. Edryd sat next to the woman and took her hand, talking in a gentle voice to calm her down.

Constable Evans made his way over to the bar and sat down next to the hunter.

"It's a bad business this," Wilson said gravely as he looked at Arwyn.

"I shouldn't be surprised that you know already," Arwyn sighed and shook his head.

"A bad business indeed," was all that Wilson said in reply.

"Something aged ten years and single malt for the lady," the constable ordered and then dropped his voice so only Alex could hear.

"I don't know if she is just seeing things in the dark or someone is playing a terrible joke, but it's not good for the festival," the constable admitted and clenched his teeth with frustration.

"I'll go fetch Pattinson from the manor, and we'll take a look in those woods for you. See what we can find," Mr Hunter said and drained his glass.

"I appreciate it," Arwyn said gratefully, his voice filled with relief. Alex nodded to his friend before he headed for the door.

"That's a bad business too," Wilson said as he came back to the bar with the whisky Constable Evans had ordered.

"What is?" Arwyn asked with confusion.

"Taken to the bottle, he has, in here every night. Drinks more than anyone else and then stumbles back to the manor after. Never brings the dog. I'd say he's taking a liking to something he can't have and now it's ruined him. Women, they're the ruin of men," Wilson said, shaking his head.

"I'll be sure to tell your Emma that," Arwyn replied coldly and turned away from the barman before he could reply.

The night outside was not cold, but nor was it warm.

There was a hint of a chill in the breeze that carried the clouds over the small village. Evening turned to night earlier and earlier now, and Alex knew that he was going to be late for dinner.

Lady Sarah pretended that his absence didn't hurt her, but he always saw the heartbreak in her eyes when he was late for dinner. Lady Sarah was not the only one who was upset with Alex's evenings out of the house. Pattinson, Alex's Akita, did not like his master's absence and was becoming more and more morose when Alex was out of the house. He spent his time lying at Lady Sarah's feet, whining at the door periodically.

When Mr Hunter did return to Grangeback, Pattinson would refuse to go near him for at least an hour, though Mrs Bosworth was certain that it would stretch to two if Mr Hunter kept up his evenings out.

Nobody in the house talked about Mr Hunter in the presence of Lady Sarah, Doctor Hales or the two Welshmen, but behind the closed doors of the servants quarters, they talked about the strange behaviour of the groundskeeper.

Cooky was disappointed in the man she had known since he was a boy. It was hardly a secret that Lady Sarah and

Mr Hunter were in love, but it now seemed that he was retreating from her and breaking the poor lady's heart.

Mrs Bosworth had become taciturn on the matter. She wouldn't talk to Mr Hunter at all, and she refused to discuss Lady Sarah and Mr Hunter with anyone else. The whole situation was starting to affect the atmosphere of the house. If it had not been for the distraction of the festival, Bosworth was certain that the manor would have become shrouded in a rather grim air. As it was, he simply had to remind the footman and maids of their duties in relation to the upcoming festival to put an end to the gossiping in the corridors.

Lady Sarah and Pattinson were sat by the fire when Mr Hunter arrived home. There was no one to greet him at the door as the guests of the household were all consumed with the final preparations for those that would be arriving at the house shortly. Lady Sarah had been excused for the preparation duties as she was feeling faint and the doctor had soothed any worries by exclaiming that she just needed to rest for a short time beside the fire.

"Where have you been?" Sarah asked as Alex walked into the room.

"In the village. Pattinson, heel," Mr Hunter

commanded. The dog looked at him with a sad expression, but got to his feet and slowly walked over to where his master stood.

"Then you know the first pickers have arrived," Sarah said without moving her eyes from the fire.

"Yes, where is everyone?" Alex replied.

"They are putting the finishing touches to our offers for the festival. The doctor excused me from helping as I felt a little faint," Sarah replied, biting her lip to keep her voice even.

"Are you alright?" Alex asked with concern but knew better than to rush to her side when she wouldn't look at him.

"I am," Lady Sarah replied shortly.

"I have to go out again," Alex said sadly.

"I see," Sarah closed her eyes and turned her head away from Alex and the fire.

"It is not what you think. A woman came running into the village, she was screaming about a witch. Edryd and Arwyn are with her at Wilson's Inn. Arwyn asked me to take Pattinson and search the woods. We will be back soon," Alex assured her.

"I will have Cooky leave your dinner in the kitchen. We expect the first of our guests tonight, and I will be going to bed not long after they arrive. You will be expected at breakfast, and every other meal whilst they are here," Sarah said coldly and slowly rose from her chair. She didn't look at the hunter at any point. Instead, she turned and calmly walked from the room, leaving Alex with nothing to do except take Pattinson out into the night.

He didn't know what he was going to do, though the easiest road for him was to simply leave the county. He would be leaving behind Lady Sarah and a baby, but the baby could be given to one of the staff and the birth hushed up. No one would have to know that he had fathered a child by Lady Sarah, and she would be free to marry someone that was acceptable in the eyes of society.

"Come on, boy," Mr Hunter sighed and took the dog out to explore the woods.

The trees around Stickleback Hollow were not as thick as once they had been, but they were not easy for most to navigate through at night. Most travellers that came to the village stuck to the paths that were well marked and well walked, even when going into the forest to search for berries. Ever since the festival had become a popular attraction, the paths to the berries had been made a lot easier to walk. There were still some spots where berries were a little harder to reach, but for the most part, the places that most people needed to reach did not require any forestry skills.

Pattinson and Mr Hunter had both spent a good deal of time in the woods and could easily move through them whether it was day or night.

Arwyn had pointed Alex in the right direction and so made his way down from the manor to the trees surrounding the road into the village instead of going back to the village first. The dog easily kept pace with his master as he strode down the slight hill into the trees.

Now he was outside with his master, Pattinson had forgiven Mr Hunter for leaving him behind at the manor. The pair searched through the trees for several hours, but there was nothing in the trees to suggest that a witch had been there. Just as Mr Hunter was about to turn to the village to report to Constable Evans, he spotted something at the foot of one of the trees. There was a pile of sulphur, and some clothes lay strewn on the ground beside it. The clothes were that of a man and boy, but they didn't look familiar to Alex.

He picked them up and whistled for Pattinson to follow him.

Arwyn was back at the police house. The woman was sat in the front room of the station, keenly waiting for news that the witch had been found. Edryd had returned to Grangeback, leaving Constable Evans with the woman and Constable Owens.

When Mr Hunter knocked on the door of the police house, the woman was the first to her feet and ran to the door. She flung it open and collapsed to her knees when she saw what Mr Hunter was carrying.

"Where did you find these?" she gasped as she pawed at the clothes.

"They were in the woods," Alex began, but he wasn't able to finish before the woman began to wail again.

"What happened?" Constable Evans asked as he came into the corridor and found the hysterical woman on the floor.

"She saw the clothes and asked where I found them," Mr Hunter said helplessly.

"They're not just clothes," she cried, "They're my son's clothes and my friend's."

"Where are they both now?" Constable Owens asked.

"They were in the woods when I ran, I haven't seen them since," the woman sobbed.

"Constable Owens, please take the lady to the front room. If you could get a description of the two missing persons and then send a message to Chester for some help. We need to find the two before the festival begins," Constable Evans said firmly. Constable Owens saluted and carefully helped the woman to her feet before leading her out of the corridor.

"Did you find any signs of a witch?" Constable Evans asked Mr Hunter when he was certain that Constable Owens and the woman were out of earshot.

"None, the only things in the woods were these clothes and what looked like a pile of sulphur," Alex shrugged.

"Sulphur?" Arwyn frowned.

"It's something I learned about in school. It's a yellow powder, well it's a chemical that can be a yellow powder. It smells like rotten eggs, it makes it easy to identify," Mr Hunter explained.

"What was it doing in the woods?" Constable Evans asked.

"That is not my department, you are the policeman. I have to go. I am late for dinner, and I want to be back at the house before Lady Sarah goes to bed," Mr Hunter sighed.

"What is troubling you both?" Constable Evans asked.

"It is complicated," Alex shook his head and began to turn away.

"You shouldn't overthink things the way you do," Arwyn said gently.

"What do you mean?" Alex frowned.

"In a place like Stickleback Hollow, a groundskeeper can marry a lady, and everyone would rejoice," Constable Evans replied.

"What about in the rest of the country?" Mr Hunter said sourly.

"The rest of the country be damned," Arwyn replied.

Chapter 10

The policemen came from Chester the next morning. However, there was no signed of the missing man or boy in the village. The woman had been taken away to Chester to the hospital at Doctor Hales' request. He had come down from the manor when Alex had returned to it and reported what had happened. The doctor was concerned at the effect that such a shock would have on the system, especially as she held fast to the belief that she had seen a witch in the woods.

There was no evidence to support her claim, though the sulphur and clothes were strange, they could have been nothing more than a practical joke.

When Mr Hunter had arrived back at Grangeback, Lady Sarah had already gone to bed, and Doctor Hales warned the hunter that she was not to be disturbed.

"She's been unwell, dear boy, she needs a good nights sleep. Smooth things over at breakfast and all will be well. She's a forgiving soul," Jack had assured him, but Alex was not so sure.

Whilst the woods were being searched, the household of Grangeback came down to breakfast. Thomas and Edward Egerton had both arrived with Charlotte Egerton and Lady Mary Pierrepont. The four were the first of the guests that were staying at Grangeback for the festival to arrive. Both Thomas and Edward could have stayed with their family at Tatton Park, but both Charlotte and Mary had wanted to stay with Lady Sarah, and the two men always strived to give their ladies what they wanted.

Mr Hunter was the first down at breakfast and waited patiently for the rest of the household before he began eating. Pattinson was lying in front of the fire, happy that his master was close at hand.

"Good morning, Hunter!" Thomas called out as he entered the dining room and firmly shook Alex by the hand. He was always pleased to see the groundskeeper, especially since Lady Sarah had arrived in Stickleback Hollow.

Mr Hunter was a quiet fellow, but he had become popular in recent years with the young men that had once bullied him at school.

They were as ignorant of his parentage as Alex had been, but his station in life had not stopped the titled young men from forming friendships with the groundskeeper.

"Good morning," Alex said as he shook hands with Thomas, then Edward, before bowing slightly to the two ladies.

"Things are certainly different since the brigadier went abroad. Where were you last night? The doctor told us you'd been called away," Edward said as he sat at the table.

"Yes, some business of a witch in the woods, but Pattinson and I couldn't find anyone," Alex managed a slight smile as he poured out tea and coffee for the guests.

"Well, that's a dramatic way to start the festival," Charlotte said with a chuckle as she sat at the table, "Now, tell us, Hunter, what is wrong with Lady Sarah? She was very quiet last night, and she seems so weak and pale!" Mrs Egerton said in a conspiratorial tone.

"She has been working hard to make the festival a success. Mrs Bosworth tells me she hasn't been sleeping well, but now that the festival is in progress, I am sure she will be back to herself in no time," Mr Hunter said with a shrug.

He knew that Lady Sarah had been feeling tired recently and the doctor had assured him that it was the pregnancy, but the pregnancy was not something the groundskeeper was about to talk to the Egertons about.

It wasn't long until the rest of the household, save for Lee and Stanley Baker, had come down for breakfast. It was a jolly affair with lots of merry talk about the events of the festival and how Lady Mary and Charlotte were looking forward to exploring the woods and looking for the witch.

Lady Sarah had remained quiet throughout the meal, smiling politely and only answering questions when they were directed to her.

Alex watched her carefully throughout the meal and could see sadness hiding behind the mask of the hostess that she wore. He knew that he was the cause of the sadness, but he had no way of making her happy either.

Just as the meal was being cleared away, Bosworth came into the dining room,

"My lady, Mr Claydon is here," the butler announced and Miss Beaumont blushed deep crimson.

"Thank you, Bosworth, ask him to join us in the parlour. We will be there in a moment," Lady Sarah said as she smiled warmly at Miss Beaumont.

"Well, if you have a visitor, we'll make our way to the village, see if we can't get a head start on the witch hunt,"

Thomas laughed.

"You would be better hunting for berries," the dean of Chester said seriously.

"Ah, come now, Mr Anson, we were just teasing Hunter. I'm actually keen for him to take us out on the lake this afternoon, if your ladyship allows," Thomas replied with a grin, addressing the last to Lady Sarah.

"Of course, though please be careful. We don't want anyone coming back cold and wet after an unseasonably cold dip in the waters," Lady Sarah joked. For a moment, her face was alive with the wry humour that Mr Hunter loved, but as quickly as it had filled her face, it was gone.

She rose from the table along with Miss Beaumont,

"I shall see you all for lunch," she said, looking pointedly at Mr Hunter before she left to greet Mr Claydon.

"Well, I hope that means that Percy will soon be busy with a wedding to prepare for," Frederick said, slapping his hand down on the edge of the table.

"You think Lady Sarah is going to get married?" Edward asked in astonishment.

"No, foolish boy, Miss Beaumont. The look on her face and the regularity with which Mr Claydon is calling. It seems to be me that wedding bells are not too far away, wouldn't you agree, Doctor?" Mr Anson asked.

"I would indeed. Mr Claydon is a man of action. If he is ready to marry, it won't be long before he proposes. But come, there is a festival to enjoy. Let us leave this breakfast gossip at the table and enjoy what the village has to offer. You might be surprised to find that there is a rather elaborate garden maze that Lady Sarah commissioned for the event. It will be open this evening, and there are prizes for those that find the centre," the doctor told the room.

Mr Hunter had been the one that had overseen the planting of the hedges to make the maze, so he knew how to navigate his way to the centre. Those that comprised the household would not be given prizes for finding the centre, but the staff had all been given a paid holiday for one day each during the festival.

Mrs Bosworth, Bosworth and Cooky had spent hours organising a rota for those days off for each of the staff so that they would not find themselves undermanned at any point. There had been a few complaints, but Mrs Bosworth had taken great care to point out that they were always free to decline the kind offer her ladyship had made if they did not want to follow the rota.

After that, there had been no complaints and the staff now all eagerly looked forward to their day of berry picking and frolics. Only one member of the staff had declined the offer, Mrs Bosworth. She too, had noticed how tired and drawn Lady Sarah had been looking in recent days. Though the doctor had assured her and Mr Hunter that it was simply part of pregnancy, Mrs Bosworth heartily disagreed.

She couldn't be certain that there was something wrong with the young lady, but until she was looking and feeling less fatigued, Mrs Bosworth was not going to be absent from the manor.

Cooky had protested, but Mrs Bosworth had silenced the clucking cook by saying,

"We have been to the festival every year since we were young. I don't need a day in the woods, and I can go with Lady Sarah when she goes to the frivolities in the evening."

Bosworth had tried to insist that he would not go to the festival if his wife was not attending, but Mrs Bosworth did not want to deprive her husband of what she knew was one of the few pleasures of life that he enjoyed outside of his work.

As Miss Beaumont and Lady Sarah met with Mr

Claydon, the first of the staff made ready to go down to the village. Thomas, Edward, Charlotte and Lady Mary were already halfway down the path, and the doctor with the dean of Chester were also putting on their coats to go out.

Edryd, Derwyn and Mr Hunter were waiting for Lady Sarah before they went down to the festival. Pattinson was quite content to sit by the fire until he was called away.

The sky was covered with clouds, but the rain was holding off as the parties from Grangeback made their way down to Stickleback Hollow.

Mr Anson and Doctor Hales took up the rear of the column, taking a more leisurely pace as they went. Lee and Stanley Baker had snuck out after wolfing down their breakfast and had made it down to Stickleback Hollow and were already on their way back to the manor, yelling for the doctor before Jack and Frederick were halfway down the driveway.

"Calm down, boys, what is all this noise about?" the doctor asked irritably.

"Miss Hales is here! She's in the village!" Lee yelled with worry. The last time Miss Hales had visited the village, he had been cuffed around the ears for being rude to her, and the memory of it still haunted him.

"Ah, dear Jessica has arrived. I expected her tomorrow, but everything should be in order. Come, Mr Anson, you'll be the first to greet my sister and the party she has brought with her," Jack said brightly.

"Where is she staying? Here at the manor?" Frederick asked and watched looks of horror appear on the Baker boys' faces.

"No, with everyone else that is visiting, there isn't room. As I am staying up here with Lady Sarah, she is staying at my home in the village. My sons should be arriving home from university today as well. They will be with us in the manner," the doctor explained.

"What a hospitable house Grangeback is," Mr Anson said with slight wonder.

"I've often said that the Webb-Kneelingroach family was the finest I have ever been acquainted with, and Lady Sarah is upholding their reputation rather beautifully," Jack beamed.

"She isn't related to the family by blood?" Mr Anson asked with surprise.

"No, she is the brigadier's ward. She grew up in India, her parents died there not that long ago. That's when she came to England. Her father served with the brigadier, and when she found London too much for her, Lady Sarah came here. She has fit in extraordinarily well, which is no mean feat in a village as – unique – as this one," the doctor said, carefully picking his words.

The doctor and dean continued to talk of the families of Webb-Kneelingroach and Montgomery Baird Watson-Wentworth as they made their way to the doctor's house.

There was no need to knock on the door, but Jack gave his sister plenty of warning as to his arrival by banging on the door three times before opening it and calling out,

"Hello the house!"

"Jack! I thought you'd be down here waiting for me!" Jessica Hales bounded into the hallway, instantly scolding her brother with her hands on her hips.

"Mr Frederick Anson, may I present my sister, Miss Jessica Hales. Dearest skin, this is Mr Frederick Anson, the new dean of Chester," the doctor said, ignoring the chiding he had received.

"A pleasure to meet you, sir. Might I introduce my companions, though not in the hallway. Come into the parlour," Jessica said as she ushered the two men into the house.

As they were herded into the parlour, they saw a middle-aged man sat upon the long sofa. He was well-dressed and had an impressive brown moustache. On the floor in front of him, two young boys were playing with a wooden train.

"May I introduce Mr Kane Taylor and his two sons, Brendan and Neil. This is my brother, Doctor Jack Hales, and Mr Frederick Anson, the dean of Chester," Miss Hales said.

"Gentlemen, a pleasure to meet you both. It is most kind of you to give us your home during our visit," Mr Taylor said as he sprang to his feet.

"You are most welcome. You aren't, perchance, related to the Taylors of Staffordshire?" the doctor asked as he shook the outstretched hand of Mr Taylor.

"I am, do you know the family?" Mr Taylor asked as he vigorously shook hands with the dean.

"Only Mr Harry Taylor," the doctor said with an air that suggested indifference.

"He's my cousin! How fortuitous! Well, I feel even happier to have made your acquaintance. I would also like to speak to you later when we are alone," Mr Taylor said in a hushed voice.

"Very well, maybe this evening at the maze at Grangeback?" the doctor asked with a slight frown. He wasn't sure why Mr Taylor wanted to speak to him alone, but he was not so rude as to decline the request.

The streets of Stickleback were filled with people when the doctor and dean stepped out of the house after only half an hour visiting with Miss Hales, Mr Taylor and his sons.

"Well, your sister is a very interesting woman," the dean said with a grin.

"She has always made life a little more intriguing," the doctor laughed.

"Laughing after meeting with Aunt Jessica? Some truly miraculous must have transpired," the voice of Richard Hales reached his father's ears. The doctor looked up to see both of his sons, Richard and Gordon, stood by the gate to the doctor's house.

"Boys, how wonderful to see you! Have you both just arrived?" Jack asked as he half-walked, half-ran down the path to greet them both.

"Yes, we thought we would walk this way to see if you were at home with Aunt Jessica before going to the manor," Gordon replied.

"Well, I am very glad you did. Boys, meet Mr Frederick Anson, dean of Chester. Frederick, these are my two sons, Richard and Gordon," the doctor said proudly.

"Very nice to meet you. Father, has there been any news of Grace or Millie?" Gordon asked earnestly.

"I'm afraid not, son, they're still looking for them," the doctor said sadly.

"I see, well, we'll go pay our respects to Hunter and Lady Sarah before we come down to the village again," Richard said solemnly and squeezed his brother's shoulder.

"Is that something that you can enlighten me on?" the Dean asked as he watched the two boys walking away.

"I can, but we will need a drink, it's a long story," Jack sighed.

"Wonderful, I have been looking forward to sampling the wares of Wilson's Inn," the dean replied, and the pair set off through the crowds so that the doctor could tell a long story without a satisfactory ending.

Chapter 11

With so many people arriving that day, Lady Sarah chose not to go down to the village. Instead, she waited to receive her guests. Mr Hunter tried to stay with her at the house, but the young lady had reminded him of Thomas and Edward's desire to go out on the lake. Alex had begrudgingly agreed to go down to the village to keep his word, and left Lady Sarah in Mrs Bosworth's care at the house.

The village was filling with people rather rapidly. It wouldn't be until the following evening when all the guests of the village would be there, but even so, Mr Hunter thought that there were far more people in the village than last year.

"Good morning, Mr Hunter," Constable Cantello said as he spotted the hunter fighting his way towards the inn.

"Good morning, Any word on the two people in the woods?" Alex asked when he was close enough to speak softly and still be heard.

"Not a sign of them. We're just having a quick bite inside before we get back out there. Feel like joining us?" the constable asked brightly.

Alex nodded and followed the policeman inside. Constable McIntyre, Clowes, McGill and Meyers were all sat around a table with Constable Evans. As Mr Hunter joined them with Constable Cantello, he reflected on how funny it was to find himself in the company of the constabulary when not that long ago they had arrested him on suspicion of murder.

The inn was full of laughter and familiar faces. Some of them were people that Alex knew from the streets of Chester. Others were young gentlemen and ladies that would be staying at Grangeback for the length of the festival.

As Alex was sat drinking with the policemen, the door to the inn opened, and Mrs Ruth Cooper entered.

The older woman had a severe look on her face. She looked briefly around and then left with the same expression she had worn when she entered.

"Well, that's not good," Mr Hunter murmured under his breath.

Mrs Ruth Cooper was not a bad woman, she was simply a woman in pain. She had lost both her husband and son in less than ideal circumstances. After the death of her husband, her son had been her pride and joy. In fact, he had become her main reason for living. He was a pampered child, but a good man none-the-less. He had once found himself interested in pursuing the attentions of Lady Sarah, but when it had become clear to him that her heart lay elsewhere, he had taken up with Miss Elizabeth Wessex instead.

Miss Wessex had once been engaged to Mr Harry Taylor, but he had broken off the engagement. Miss Wessex never knew the reasons behind Harry's decision, as the young man had kept those to himself.

He had broken off the engagement because it had become clear to him that Miss Wessex was not suited to a life in the service of one such as Lady de Mandeville. Rather than prolong an engagement that would never lead to marriage, Harry had cut the girl loose so that she had a chance to find happiness somewhere else.

It had broken his heart to do so, but it had been a necessity, and it had not taken long for Mr Daniel Cooper and Miss Elizabeth Wessex to find one another.

The pair had become engaged extremely quickly, and when Daniel had been found murderer, Mrs Ruth Cooper had laid the blame at the feet of Miss Wessex, especially as Daniel had recently changed his will to leave his fortune and Duffleton Hall to Miss Wessex.

Mrs Ruth Cooper had been left an allowance, but it was barely enough for a woman in her position to get by on. The only reason she was surviving was the charity and hospitality of the Egerton family of Tatton Park.

It wasn't long after Mrs Cooper's appearance at the inn that Thomas, Edward, Charlotte and Lady Mary arrived, ready to take Mr Hunter out on the lake – or rather ready for Mr Hunter to row the party about on the lake.

Richard and Gordon Hales came in a few moments later, and the party swelled from five to seven. There was lots of back-patting, and the four gentlemen very eagerly made the acquaintance of the policemen that Alex was drinking with, though Alex and the constables knew they had all met before.

"I shall see you later," Alex said with a slight sigh as he stood from the table and was half-pushed, half-dragged out of the inn by the two ladies, eager not to miss the sunset.

The constables laughed and cheered the sight of the two petite ladies manhandling the giant hunter.

Making their way through Stickleback Hollow and through the edge of the forest was quite difficult with the number of people crowding the streets. Constable Owens was patrolling, ensuring that no one was causing any trouble. Mr Hunter knew that he was given the duty as a hazing exercise by the other policeman, but he still seemed capable enough, even if he had already alienated half the village.

As he pushed through the throng, he spied Derwyn leaning against the frame of one of the stalls talking to a rather beautiful looking woman. She wasn't dressed too lavishly, but all her clothing hinted at a level of wealth.

Gordon saw the hunter staring and shouted above the noise to be heard,

"That's Katherine DeVille. She's somewhat newly arrived to society. Her father is some kind of farmer from Scotland that's been given a title for some reason or another. Not really clear on the details, but she's using her mother's name to avoid being too closely connected with the man," the son of the doctor explained.

"Well she can't have too much against farming since she's talking to Derwyn," Mr Hunter replied with a slight grin. Gordon clapped his hand on his friend's shoulder in a gesture of agreement.

It took twenty minutes of pushing for the group to

finally break away from the throng of people.

"What a relief," Lady Mary sighed.

"We won't have to push like that on the way back too, will we?" Charlotte asked Alex.

"No, we'll take the path to the manor," Mr Hunter replied.

"Did our apologies over not attending lunch reach the manor? We got so swept up the festival stalls, we quite lost track of time," Edward said as the group followed Alex through the trees to the water's edge.

"They did. Lady Sarah was not offended," Mr Hunter replied a little more shortly than he had intended.

"Good, good, now let's get out on that water!" Thomas said, clapping his hands.

Alex led the group to the old lodge where he lived when he wasn't invited to stay at Grangeback. It was a nice enough building, a little small for a man of his size, but the hunter had grown used to his home over the years.

Not far beyond the lodge was a boathouse. The boathouse had a number of different rowboats and a small sailing boat inside it, all of which belonged to the manor.

"We'll take two boats, none of them are big enough for

all of us," Alex announced. Thomas and Edward looked worried for a moment, but Richard stepped forward to take up the rowing duties in the second boat.

"I think I'll take the sailboat out if you don't mind," Gordon said as he looked over the craft.

"Not at all. Thomas and Charlotte can go with Richard in this boat," Alex said as he pointed to one on the left side of the small jetty, "Edward and Lady Mary can come with me in this boat," he finished by pointing to a rowboat on the right side of the small jetty.

He opened the doors to the boathouse as Richard and Gordon helped the Egerton party into their respective boats. Lines were cast off, and soon all three boats were moving across the water of the lake.

Gordon and Richard had spent no small amount of time on the water in their youth. They were well acquainted with the lake and the dangerous shallows that hid at different points, waiting to ensnare unsuspecting sailors.

Gordon unfurled the small sail, and though there was only a light wind, he easily and quickly sailed across the water, crossing the path of Richard's boat to wow Charlotte and annoy his brother.

It was a pleasant enough distraction. The sun began to set and sent pinks and oranges streaking across the sky. Through the trees, the berry pickers could be seen examining the bushes and rushing past other people trying to find the juiciest berries.

Lady Mary was looking down at the water, looking for fish coming to the surface to eat the insects that were hovering over it. Edward was watching the young lady with a smile on his face that Alex found very familiar.

It was the same smile that he wore when he sat and watched Lady Sarah when she didn't know that Mr Hunter was looking at her. The look made his thoughts drift to Lady Sarah and her pregnancy. He felt like a fool for thinking that he had to leave the lady and have her baby raised by the household staff instead of its parents.

Before he could think any further on his problem, Lady Mary screamed. She threw herself back from the edge of the boat and almost fell over the other side. The boat rocked from side to side, and for a moment Alex was worried that the boat was going to capsize.

"What's wrong?" Edward asked as he tried to calm down Lady Mary without causing the boat to rock any more than it already was.

"There's a man in the water," Lady Mary gasped. She was pale and shaking. Mr Hunter looked at Lady Mary and risked a look over the side.

Floating in the water was the body of a man without any clothes on, and beside him was the floating body of a boy.

"Richard, Gordon, we need to go back," Alex shouted and turned the boat back towards the boathouse.

Mr Hunter waited with the Egerton party, and Gordon whilst Richard ran back to Stickleback Hollow to fetch the police. By the time the police arrived at the lake, it was getting dark.

Constable McGill and Constable Clowes rowed out into the lake with lanterns on hooks so that they could find the bodies and fish them out of the water.

"With the clothes we found in the forest and their bodies in the water, they must have tried to swim across the lake and lost their way in the dark. Unable to find their way back to the shore, they drowned," Constable McIntyre said, trying to convince himself as he spoke.

"I suppose so," Mr Hunter shrugged. He knew that the policeman didn't really believe the story that he had invented, but there was no other explanation to be had, unless there really was a witch.

The thought made the hairs on the back of Alex's neck stand on end, but his biggest concern was that he and the rest of the party were now all late for dinner.

Chapter 12

Once the bodies had been brought in from the lake, people were once again allowed to go out on the water. Boats from the village had been brought down to the water's edge and lay for the general use of the berry pickers. Lanterns were lit and placed all around the edge of the lake, and special poles with hooks had been fixed on the boats for people to hand lanterns from them when they were out on the water.

Alex led a shocked Lady Mary, Charlotte, Thomas, Edward, Richard and Gordon back to Grangeback along a path that led straight to the house and hoped that rumour had raced ahead of them and explained their absence.

When they reached the manor, Lady Mary had stopped shaking. The distance they were from the lake seemed to be helping to lift her spirits. Mrs Bosworth was waiting on the steps and bundled Lady Mary and Charlotte into the house in a motherly fashion.

"Are you alright?" Lady Sarah asked softly of Alex. She was stood in the doorway to the brigadier's study. Richard and

Gordon had gone in search of food in the kitchens, whilst Thomas and Edward had gone after Mrs Bosworth and the two ladies. This had left the hunter alone in the hallway.

"Just a nasty shock for the ladies, dead bodies are all the same to me," Alex shrugged, "I sorry we missed dinner," he said awkwardly, "and that I've been so distant."

"Is there something we need to talk about?" Lady Sarah asked sadly.

"No, not yet at least. With the maze opening tonight, you have bigger concerns," Mr Hunter smiled warmly at the lady and reached out to take her hand.

"Come to the kitchen, Cooky has been keeping food warm for you, and I am sure that Pattinson will be getting under her feet by now," Lady Sarah said as she took the hunter's hand.

"I love you," Alex said softly as he gently brushed a hair out of Sarah's eyes.

"I love you too," she replied.

The sound of Cooky yelling echoed down the hallway as the pair approached the kitchens. Richard and Gordon were causing havoc along with Pattinson, so much so that upon entering the kitchen, both Alex and Lady Sarah burst into laughter.

"You!" Cooky shouted, narrowing her eyes at Alex, "Call off your damn dog."

"Pattinson, heel boy," Alex gasped as he stopped laughing. The dog perked up his ears but didn't respond, "HEEL," Alex growled, and the Japanese hunting dog whined as he padded his way over to where Alex and Sarah stood.

"Hunter, here, there's a rather good pork pie that Cooky was trying to hide from us," Gordon said as he held the plate over his head and out of Cooky's reach.

"Yes, come grab a piece, and we can go down to the maze. Charlotte and Mary will be with father for a while, so let's see if we can't get to the centre and win a prize without them," Richard said as he took a slice of the pie off the plate and threw it towards Mr Hunter.

Alex caught the piece of pie and bit into it before Cooky could protest.

"It's very good," Mr Hunter said approvingly, and Cooky blushed.

"Hand that plate over now. You may be the sons of the doctor, but you aren't too big for me to take a broom to you both," Cooky said, trying to sound angry, but it was clear that she was enjoying the attention the boys were giving her. It was not often that she had compliments given to her cooking by guests at the house, and it was even rarer that they would be eating in the kitchen.

Richard and Gordon looked at each other before Gordon gave the plate to Cooky and the two boys planted a kiss on either cheek of the cook.

"You're a good sport, Cooky," Richard said.

"Come on, Hunter, last to the centre buys the beer," Gordon challenged, and the brothers raced out of the kitchen door before Cooky could react to their kisses.

"Those boys, they never change," Cooky said, clearly flustered.

"You put up with so much, Cooky," Lady Sarah consoled the cook.

"They're not a bad sort though," Cooky sighed and rubbed both her cheeks with her apron.

"Mr Hunter, kindly make sure they don't get into any more trouble," Lady Sarah said, and Alex nodded, setting off after the Hales boys with Pattinson at his heel.

"I must go and open the maze as part of the festival, Cooky, could you ensure that both Mr Egertons, Mrs Egerton and Lady Pierrepont are fed?" Lady Sarah asked as Cooky straighten herself up.

"Of course, my lady," Cooky said, feeling much better now the chaos in the kitchen had ended.

"Thank you, I will make sure that the doctor sends his sons to accompany their aunt round the village tomorrow – to make amends for all the trouble they caused you," Lady Sarah winked at the cook, and Cooky laughed with delight.

As Lady Sarah stepped out of the kitchen door, the sound of voices greeted her.

The hedge maze was one of the biggest attractions of the festival, and already there were crowds of people waiting for her ladyship to official open it.

Bosworth had assigned a group of footmen to stand on guard at the maze entrance to stop anyone going into it before it was opened and gaining an advantage over everyone else in the hunt for the prize at the centre.

Not all of the people in the village for the festival were waiting outside of the maze, some were taking advantage of the crowd drawer and walking the quieter forest in search of berries. Lanterns had not only be placed around the lake and on the boats, but lines of them marked the main berry trails through the woods.

The maze was also lit with lanterns, so much so that some remarked that more money seemed to have been spent on the ironwork than on anything else.

Lady Sarah had been the one to pay for all the lanterns and Mr Fletcher, the blacksmith, had made them. As far as the two of them were concerned, the lanterns were an investment in the festival, something that would be needed for many years to come and something that was necessary for the success of the festival.

Richard and Gordon had managed to push their way to the front of the throng and eagerly waited as Lady Sarah slowly made her way to the footmen at the maze entrance.

"Thank you all for coming. As you know, this maze has a prize at the centre of it. The first person or party to reach the centre will win that prize, but the maze is not a simple one to navigate. If you get lost and cannot find your way back, never fear, the footmen know the maze and will be walking around it and ready to guide you out should you need help. Remember that the maze is supposed to be fun and all that reach the centre will receive something for their efforts – even if they are not the first. With that, I declare the Grangeback Hedge Maze, open!" Lady Sarah said. Her voice was not as powerful as it normally was, but it still carried over the crowd, and a great cheer rose up as the footmen stood to the side and the people rushed forward into the maze.

As the people pressed forward, Lady Sarah was overcome with a wave of dizziness, and Alex had to move quickly to catch her before she fell to the ground.

"What is it?" Alex frowned as he held the woman in his arms.

"Nothing, I suddenly felt a little unwell. Maybe I should return to the house," Sarah smiled weakly at him, and Alex turned from the throng and carried the lady back to her home.

He went in through the kitchen, Pattinson still trotting at his heel.

"Oh! Your ladyship!" Cooky fussed as Alex strode through the kitchen.

"Cooky, if you could send the doctor to Lady Sarah's room once he has finished with the other ladies," Mr Hunter asked, ignoring the flapping the cook was doing. He didn't wait for an answer, but continued his stride, not breaking it until he reached Lady Sarah's room and laid her on her bed.

"There's no need to fuss," Lady Sarah soothed, trying

to get out of the bed, but Mr Hunter placed his hand on her shoulder and stopped her.

"There is every need to fuss. Now lie down until the doctor tells you that it is safe to leave the bed," Mr Hunter said sternly.

The two waited in silence for half an hour before the doctor arrived.

"Ah, my lady, feeling a little faint, are we?" Doctor Jack Hales asked as he entered the room.

"I'll wait downstairs," Mr Hunter said and left the doctor alone to examine the lady. As he descended to the hallway below, he could hear Stanley and Lee Baker yelling and Mrs Bosworth trying to calm them down.

"What's going on?" Alex asked with a frown as he reached the foot of the stairs.

"Mr Hunter! It's the witch! She's in the woods!" Lee said, rushing over to the hunter.

"There is no witch," Mr Hunter said with a sigh.

"No! There is! Lots of people saw her near the lake. They're saying she took a boat of people right in front of them," Stanley continued chattering.

"Both of you stay here with Mrs Bosworth. I will go and

see what I can find," Alex said firmly. Pattinson was already waiting at the door, his tail wagging.

Alex walked sedately down the path whilst he could be seen from the windows of the house, but as soon as he knew he could not be seen, he set off running. He ran with almost reckless abandon down to the lake. He was nearly out of breath when he found the police constables circling the lake.

"I see Lee and Stanley Baker are spreading news with their usual alacrity," Arwyn said dryly as he saw Alex appear.

"Who is missing?" Mr   Hunter asked worriedly.

"We don't have any names, all we know is that a man, woman and boy were in the boat on the lake. The boat has disappeared, but we're waiting until morning until we go out to look for them," Constable McGill said slowly.

"Is there anything I can help with?" Alex asked.

"Maybe, Mrs Cooper is making a lot of noise in the inn, she isn't listening to Constable Owens or Clowes, but she may listen to you," Constable McIntyre shrugged.

"I doubt it, but if you are not going out onto the water until the morning, then it is better than doing nothing," Mr Hunter shrugged.

"I'll come with you," Constable Meyers volunteered.

Alex nodded, and the pair set off towards the village and Wilson's Inn.

The woods had taken on a rather ill-feeling in the last day, and disappearances connected with the lake was not going to help people feel safe or relaxed whilst picking berries, especially in the twilight.

As they approached the inn, they could hear Mrs Cooper yelling at the top of her lungs. Opening the door, the inn was all but deserted, save for the two constables and the barman.

"You, Hunter, you listen to me. I know who this witch is and these fools won't listen," Mrs Cooper cried as she laid eyes on Alex and came marching over to him.

"What won't they listen to?" Mr Hunter asked impatiently. He had very little time for the woman, no matter how much she had lost, she was an irritable and argumentative creature.

"The witch is Miss Wessex. No one has been allowed to stay at Duffleton Hall during this festival, and she hasn't shown her face down her either. She is the one who was responsible for the death of my son, and she stole my home away from me. Now she is up at the hall, hiding away and practising her dark arts," Mrs Cooper said with conviction.

"What do you expect to be done about her?" Alex asked with a raised eyebrow.

"Go to her house! Make her come down to the village, show everyone the witch that she is," Mrs Cooper said firmly.

"Very well, Constable Meyers will come with me," Alex sighed.

"Now?" Constable Meyers asked with a small measure of surprise.

"Yes, the sooner we go, the sooner things will quieten down," Alex assured him.

"There are some horses that you can use outside," Wilson said to the pair as they turned to go outside.

On foot, it would take the men a few hours to reach Duffleton Hall and come back again, on horseback it would take much less.

The two rode at a trot, keeping to one side of the road to avoid the people in the village until they were clear and on the path that led through the woods and up to Duffleton Hall.

It was completely dark by the time they reached the great house, and Constable Meyers was not looking forward to riding back through the woods in the dead of night.

Alex had the constable remain on his horse and hold the reins of Alex's horse whilst he went to enquire at the house. The hunter knew that Miss Wessex would not be pleased with being dragged down to the village at such a late hour, but it was better than having Mrs Ruth Cooper barracking on about the girl for days.

He knocked firmly on the front door of the house and waited. It didn't take long for the butler to answer.

"Can I help you, sir?" the butler asked as he sneered at the groundskeeper.

"Miss Wessex is required to come down to Stickleback Hollow on police business," Mr Hunter said firmly and stood to one side so that the butler could see the police constable that was waiting on his horse.

"I'm sorry, sir, but Miss Wessex is not here," the butler's manner had changed completely.

"Where is she?" Alex asked.

"No one knows. We thought she had gone down to Stickleback Hollow for the festival. We haven't seen her for days now. Oh my, something must have happened to her," the butler's voice had a rising tone of alarm to it.

"I think you should come to the village with us," Alex

said calmly, and the butler merely nodded.

Chapter 18

Stickleback Hollow had sombre mood cast over it as Mr Hunter, Constable Meyers and the butler from Duffleton Hall rode down to it. The missing people and rumours of a witch meant that the evening festivities had been called off and people were now either tucked up in bed behind locked doors, clutching bibles, or sat in the common room of Wilson's Inn slowly sipping from heavy drinks.

As soon as Mr Hunter had agreed to go and fetch Miss Wessex, Mrs Ruth Cooper had calmed down and sat as dulcet as a lamb in the corner of the inn.

Constable Meyers took the butler to the police house, whilst Mr Hunter went to fetch Constables Evans, Cantello and McGill. He thought it best to leave Constable Owens with Mrs Cooper and Constable McIntyre guarding the lake.

There was not much the butler could tell the policemen, but it was clear that the mystery around the festival's disappearances was growing.

"It can't really be a witch, can it?" Arwyn asked Alex as

Constables Meyers and Cantello escorted the butler back to Duffleton Hall, and Constable McGill went to help Constable McIntyre guard the lake.

"There are more things in heaven and earth, Horatio, than are dreamt of in your philosophies," Mr Hunter replied with the quote he had learned at school. Arwyn looked at him with a quizzical expression, "I guess it means that anything is possible, and though we may think it unlikely, we cannot say that there is not a witch until we know otherwise," Alex shrugged.

"You better keep those thoughts to yourself, if anyone else starts thinking that, then we'll not only have a panic to deal with, but the festival will be cut short. That's something that a lot of the businesses in the village can't afford," Constable Evans warned his friend.

"Then I suppose we better find out who is causing all these problems then," Mr Hunter replied with a wry smile.

"Not tonight though, I need a few hours sleep before I go and take over from McGill and McIntyre. McGill will tell McIntyre what the butler told us. I'd rather we kept Owens out of the loop for the moment. Leave him babysitting Mrs Cooper," Arwyn sighed.

"You don't like him, do you?" Alex asked with amusement.

"Not one bit, but I suppose I'll have to make the best of it," Arwyn sighed and shrugged.

"Get some rest, my friend," Alex said warmly.

"Give my regards to Lady Sarah," Arwyn replied and began to climb the stairs to his bed.

Mr Hunter left the police house and quietly shut the door behind him.

Whatever was going on, it was clear that someone was trying to sabotage the festival. Whether it was someone with a grudge against the whole village or just one person in Stickleback Hollow, Alex didn't know, but he was certain that he would find out.

He moved quickly, Pattinson keeping pace with his master. The dog had been on quite the adventure already that night, it was rare that he would take the dog as far as Duffleton and back, but Pattinson had seen content enough with the run, and Mr Hunter was certain that the dog would sleep well that night.

He was glad not to be alone as he climbed up through the trees to reach the manor. Even though he knew the woods and trees around the Grangeback estate better than any man alive, his mind was still playing tricks on him, and every shadow held the promise of danger.

Pattinson was above such petty trifles as his mind playing games. He saw only real dangers, whether they were supernatural or not, Alex knew that as long as Pattinson's fur remained flat and the dog wasn't growling, they were both safe.

When he finally reached Grangeback, he expected to find the house in darkness with only a light left outside to guide him home, yet the lights were light in the hallway and the upper rooms at the front of the house.

Mr Hunter opened the door to find the servants all gathered in the hallway with concerned looks on their faces.

"What's happened?" Alex asked of Bosworth as he came through the door.

"It's Lady Sarah. She woke up screaming in pain. The doctor is with her now," Bosworth said. The butler was clearly very worried but was doing his best to look calm for the sake of the rest of the household.

"Then all is being done that can be, everyone should go back to bed. I will stay up and talk to the doctor. If there is any news, I will come and wake you," Mr Hunter promised. The staff looked at one another and then at Mrs Bosworth.

The housekeeper regarded Alex with narrowed eyes as she considered the wisdom of what he said. Then nodded her head slightly in agreement. The staff all began to disperse, mumbling to one another as they went.

"Sir, if I may stay up with you? I will make up a tea tray," Bosworth said helpfully.

"Thank you, Bosworth," Mr Hunter said and patted the family retainer on the shoulder.

Alex climbed the stairs slowly. He wasn't sure what he would find when he reached Lady Sarah's room, he only knew that he was filled with dread at the idea of her being ill.

He quietly opened the door to Lady Sarah's room, and Pattinson pushed past him. The dog whined as he jumped onto the bed and curled up with Lady Sarah. The blankets and sheets were covered with muddy paw prints, but Pattinson was completely unconcerned with the mess. His concern was all focused on Lady Sarah.

She was lying in bed looking paler than ever, her breathing was shallow, and sweat covered her brow, but she was asleep now.

"How is she?" Mr Hunter whispered to the doctor who sat by her bedside.

"In no immediate danger," the doctor assured him, "it is proving a difficult pregnancy for her. I've done what I can to make her comfortable, and she should feel better in the morning. She would be best staying in bed for a few days and resting to recover her strength, but it may be more than I can do to keep her there," Jack shrugged, "You best to bed, I will call you if anything changes."

"Thank you," Alex sighed with relief.

"Oh, Mr Hunter," the doctor said softly.

"Yes?"

"No one would think any less of either of you for marrying without the permission of the brigadier," Jack said pointedly.

"Thank you," Mr Hunter replied, and leaving Pattinson to watch over the woman he loved, the groundskeeper went downstairs.

"How is she, sir?" Bosworth asked as Alex descended.

"Sleeping. The doctor is with her still, but he thinks she will be fine. Just needs some bed rest for a few days," Alex smiled weakly.

"I have put the tea in the study. Mr Evans senior is also in there. I will be in the kitchen should you need me. Mrs Bosworth and Cooky are also there," Bosworth said and bowed slightly before disappearing back down the hall.

The house stood in relative darkness now, except for a lamp at the foot of the stairs, a light from the kitchen and a light cast through the open door of the brigadier's study.

Mr Hunter made his way into the study and found Edryd pouring out tea for the pair of them.

"I couldn't sleep," the older Welshman shrugged.

"Thoughts of witches or young women ensnaring your son?" Alex asked, only half-teasing the older man.

"So you've seen her too? She seems to have taken control of Derwyn's mind. If there was ever a witch in a place, then she'd go around doing that, not snatching people and boats off lakes," Edryd snorted.

"Perhaps, though I imagine she isn't a bad prospect for Derwyn," Alex shrugged as he sat down in George's chair behind the desk and took one of the cups of tea.

"She's far too pretty to be happy as a farmer's wife, too pretty by far," Edryd said darkly.

"Farmer's don't deserve pretty wives?" Mr Hunter

asked with amazement.

"Farming isn't the province of pretty women. They want trinkets and clothes, to be seen at parties and in society. Farmers need to work the land and stay as far from the nonsense of the cities as they can. Pretty women don't do well in the solitude. My wife is a handsome woman, but she's not a pretty creature with a head full of lace," Edryd explained.

"And they aren't the type to help with lambing, I suppose," Alex finished the thought.

"I've never seen a pretty woman in a sty or stable, let alone helping with the lambing. It's all too dirty a business for them," Edryd said, shaking his head.

"She is a farmer's daughter though, she'll know what life on a farm is like," Mr Hunter countered.

"And a life she'll want to avoid no doubt, no Derwyn will be better off finding a girl back in the Welsh countryside, not an English farmer's daughter," Edryd said firmly.

"So it's the English that's bothering you," Alex laughed and almost dropped his teacup.

"Aye, well, maybe, but she's still too pretty," Edryd huffed.

"Well, even if she is, she's got her hooks in Derwyn

right now," Mr Hunter grinned.

"How is the witch hunt going?" Edryd asked, changing the subject.

"It's all rumour so far. It's not like there isn't precedence for witchcraft here, it's just been a few hundred years since we last had a witch here," Alex shrugged.

"You really think there could be one?" Edryd sounded surprised.

"Anything is possible, though, without any proof, it will just lead to panic," Alex replied.

"Where did the witches live last time there were here?" Edryd asked.

"They lived down in Stickleback Hollow amongst the normal people, well, whatever passes for normal in Stickleback Hollow. But the practised their arts on the top of the Edge. It's supposedly the site of power for dark forces as a great army that a wizard assembled sleeps beneath the Edge, waiting to rise to defend England in its hour of need. With some many men and horses on noble heart sleeping underneath, dark forces can draw on their life energy and become more powerful – at least that is how the legend goes," Mr Hunter replied with a heavy sigh.

"Then perhaps we should go and see if there any signs up there of a witch, but maybe we wait until it is light," Edryd said, glancing out of the window at the darkness of the night outside.

"A very good idea indeed," Alex replied, and the two men settle down to finish their tea.

Chapter 14

Lady Sarah slept soundly through the rest of the night. She felt stronger when dawn arrived, but Doctor Hales insisted that she remain in bed.

Charlotte and Lady Mary had both decided that they had seen enough of the festival and went to Lady Sarah's room to keep the sick woman company whilst the rest of the household and its guests went down to the village.

No one had found the centre of the maze on the first night, though Richard and Gordon Hales were both determined to be the first. As soon as breakfast was over, the pair rushed out to try and beat others to the centre.

With more the young gentlemen of Cheshire in the house, Thomas and Edward were in their element, organising all of the young men into parties to get the most of our berries in the woods.

Derwyn had not been seen at breakfast, but there was so much excitement that he wasn't missed, and neither were Edryd, Alex or Pattinson.

Mr Evans senior and Mr Hunter had risen before even Cooky had woken up, though the pair had found her asleep by the fire in the kitchen when they went down to steal some bread and jam for breakfast before they left on their trip to the edge.

As Lady Sarah was confined to her bed, Black Guy was free for Mr Evans to ride and Mr Hunter could ride his own horse, Harald. The pair were Friesians that the Brigadier Webb-Kneelingroach had bought when Lady Sarah had come to live at Grangeback. Originally Harald had been George's horse, but as she and Alex had become inseparable, George had quickly given his horse to the young hunter.

Pattinson seemed to have recovered from all the running he had done the day before and had spent a rather comfortable night on the bed of Lady Sarah. Mr Hunter knew that he would have to apologise to Mrs Bosworth when they got back, but as she wasn't talking to him at the moment, it was an apology that could wait.

There were very few people out of the road that ran up to Grangeback that morning, aside from Mr Martin Ferguson, the baker, Mr Henry Boult, the fishmonger, Mr Ross Pick, the greengrocer, Mr S. Carter, the butcher and Mr Colin Nicholls, the bookseller.

The last was not surprising, though he was a man that generally never left his store, upon hearing Lady Sarah was ill, he had set out with a number of books that the lady might find entertaining whilst she was forced to rest in bed.

It was something that he did for the richer people in the neighbourhood as he could guarantee that he would sell more books in a short space of time to bedridden ladies than he would in a week of standing behind his shop counter.

Lady Sarah was a frequent customer in his store, so the bookseller was aware of the reading tastes of the young lady and carried six books with him that he was certain that the lady would enjoy.

The other tradesmen were riding on carts that were piled high with food for the house. Cooky had been ordering daily deliveries to cope with the number of people staying in the house, and the tradesmen were only too happy to fill the orders.

It seemed that in the bright light of the cool autumn day that all thoughts of the witch had been banished. People were rising from their beds and stepping out onto the street with a renewed energy. By the time Edryd and Alex reached the village, the streets were as busy as they had been the day before.

People jostled one another to get to market stalls and to be the first to reach new spots in the woods. As the pair moved slowly through Stickleback Hollow, they saw Miss Katherine DeVille and Derwyn moving from stall to stall, arm in arm. Edryd made a face, and Mr Hunter couldn't help but laugh at the expression.

"It could be worse," Alex called back to the Welshman.

"How?" Edryd asked grumpily.

"She could be Scottish," Mr Hunter laughed.

"It would be better if she were!" Edryd didn't find the thought funny at all.

There were other familiar faces out on the street that day, though Mrs Ruth Cooper was thankfully not among them. Miss Beaumont and Mr Claydon were walking about the village hand-in-hand, not far behind Miss DeVille and Derwyn. Between the two couples, Lee and Stanley Baker walked.

Mr Hunter felt slightly ashamed that he had not spent much time with the two boys over the last few months, but he promised himself that he would make it up to the two boys by offering to apprentice them both.

They seemed happy enough to explore the festival in the company of Derwyn and Miss Beaumont and their partners. When the two boys spied Mr Hunter on the back of the horse, their faces lit up, and they pushed forward to tell the hunter everything they were going to do during the day.

"Oh, father, where are you going?" Derwyn asked, seeing his father for the first time as he tore his eyes away from Miss DeVille.

"Mr Hunter and I are going into the woods towards the Edge, we shouldn't be too long. The horses needed exercising," Edryd said with a strained expression on his face.

"I see. Father, I'd like you to meet Miss Katherine DeVille. Miss DeVille, this is my father, Mr Edryd Evans and my friend, Mr Alexander Hunter of Grangeback.," Derwyn said nervously.

"A pleasure," Miss DeVille said politely. She smiled at the two men, but her smile didn't reach her eyes. She regarded both men with disdain, though she tried her best to mask it with her smile, " Derwyn tells me that you are own a sizeable farm spread in Wales."

"My son says many things. If you'll excuse us, we have to exercise the horses and return to Grangeback. Her ladyship is expecting us for lunch," Edryd said firmly.

"Ah, Edryd, a moment if you will. You too, Hunter," Mr Claydon called out, "Excuse me a moment, Miss Beaumont. I will not belong. Perhaps you, Derwyn and Miss DeVille could take Stanley and Lee to the apple bobbing, and I will join you there in a moment," the explorer made the suggestion, which was immediately seized upon by the two boys who grabbed the hands of the adults and began to drag them through the crowds.

"A private word is it, Mitchell?" Alex teased as he leaned forward in his saddle.

"Yes, well, it's a sensitive matter," Mr Claydon said as he wrung his hands together.

"You want us to come with you to take you to Lady Sarah this afternoon to ask a certain question?" Edryd asked coyly.

"Is it that obvious?" Mr Claydon asked with a sigh.

"It is, but that is no bad thing," Alex replied warmly.

"We'll call on the way back for you," Edryd assured the explorer, and the two horsemen set off towards the Edge.

There was nothing in the woods to suggest that there was anything amiss as they rode. The day was pleasant, and everyone they passed in the trees was busy with berry collecting.

The Edge was an interesting formation. It rose up to tower over Stickleback Hollow and was the source of many legends. In the years before the village had become mostly a farming community, there had been a mine that had provided tin to the local community. The mine was long abandoned now, and druids started using the site as a place to conduct ceremonies. It had been cleared out by the men of the village before Mr Hunter had been born, and it was part of Mr Hunter's job as groundskeeper at Grangeback to ensure that the site remained free of druids and witchcraft.

He had been so distracted by his predicament with Lady Sarah that he had not thought to check the Edge for any signs of the supposed witch.

Once they were out of the village, it didn't take long for the pair to reach the top of the Edge. It was an easy ride and much faster on horseback than it would have been on foot.

They dismounted just before the crest of the rise and tied the horses to one of the trees. It would be easier to search the area on foot than looking down at it from atop a horse.

Almost immediately, Mr Hunter could see that

something was wrong.

He walked towards the mouth of the mine and stopped to survey the ground around him.

"What is it?" Edryd asked as he watched the hunter move.

"Someone has been moving rocks around here. They seem to be arranged in a pattern, but I can't tell what it is from here," Alex said with a frown.

"What if we looked at it from on top of the mine entrance?" Edryd suggested.

A moment later, the two men were scrambling on top of the mine entrance and looking down at the pattern.

"That is impossible," Edryd gasped.

The stones before the men hand all been arranged to form a pentagram with an altar at the centre of it.

"We need to destroy this," Alex said firmly, but before the two men could move, the sound of a child screaming began to echo through the trees.

Chapter 15

Mr Hunter and Mr Evans Senior didn't hesitate. They ran down from the top of the mine entrance, pulled their horses' reins free and sprang into their saddles.

Black Guy and Harald responded to the urgency in their riders' movements. The cantered, sure-footed, over the uneven ground. Though Edryd was concerned about what had happened to make the child cry, he didn't know what Mr Hunter did.

If they could hear the child crying on the Edge, it was too far from the village to be heard.

It felt like an eternity, but the ride was very short. They soon came across a young boy sat at the foot of a tree crying. Around him were three piles of clothes.

"These look like Jessica's clothes," Edryd said as he dismounted and picked up the woman's clothes from the ground.

Alex moved past the clothes and got off Harald to kneel beside the young boy. Upon seeing the man, the boy threw himself at Mr Hunter, wrapping his arms around the hunter's neck and crying even harder than before.

"Gather the clothes, we'll take him to Grangeback. You can send for Arwyn when he is safe there," Mr Hunter said, and Edryd didn't argue with him.

Chapter 16

The boy didn't stop crying as they rode back to the house. Mr Hunter took them on a route that skirted the village to avoid coming across too many people and causing a panic.

The sound of the boy weeping was so loud that those in Grangeback could hear the three approaching and were waiting outside when they arrived.

Mrs Bosworth looked horrified at seeing the state the child was in and instantly whisked the screaming boy into the house to calm him down.

"I'll go and fetch Arwyn and show him the clothes. I think you should be gentle when you talk to the doctor," Edryd said to Alex, turned Black Guy away from the house and rode back down to Stickleback Hollow.

Alex took Harald to the stables and left the horse in the care of the stable boys. He went into the house through the kitchen and found the boy sitting in Mrs Bosworth's lap. He had stopped crying, but he was clearly in shock.

"What is all the commotion?" Doctor Hales asked as he

came into the kitchen. Before anyone he could answer them he saw the boy on Mrs Bosworth's knee, "Neil? What are you doing here? Where is your father? Where is Jessica?"

At the mention of Miss Hales and his father, Neil burst into tears again.

"We found him in the forest, only the clothes of his brother, father and Miss Hales were with him," Alex explained gently as he watched the colour drain from the doctor's face.

"The witch? The witch has taken my sister?" the doctor gasped and almost collapsed. Alex caught the man whilst Cooky fetched a chair for the doctor to sit on.

With the doctor in the care of Cooky and Neil being cared for by Mrs Bosworth, Mr Hunter was free to go to Lady Sarah's side.

The altar built on the Edge and more people disappearing had forced Alex to make a decision. He knew what he had to do, no matter what the consequences were.

He knocked on the door to her room and waited for permission to enter. He didn't know whether Lady Mary and Charlotte were still in Lady Sarah's room, and he had no desire to burst in on the three women.

"Enter," Lady Sarah's voice drifted through the door.

Alex gingerly opened the door and saw the young lady was lying in bed reading. Lady Mary and Charlotte were nowhere in sight.

"Sarah," Alex said as he shut the door behind her, "There is something we need to talk about."

Lady Sarah's heart stopped in her chest. She had been dreading the conversation that she felt approaching.

"Very well," she said as she closed her book and folded her hands in her lap.

"Marry me," Mr Hunter blurted out. In his head, he had prepared an elaborate speech about how much he loved her and how he didn't care what anyone else thought about their relationship. But all that it came to was two words he couldn't keep himself from saying.

Lady Sarah sat on her bed, completely speechless. She had been expecting a completely different conversation, and the two words Mr Hunter had spoken rang in her ears.

The silence between the pair seemed to drag on for hours for Alex as he stood waiting for an answer.

"Marry you?" Lady Sarah repeated.

"Yes," Alex said earnestly.

"Yes," Lady Sarah replied with a broad grin.

"Yes?" Mr Hunter asked in disbelief.

"Yes!" Lady Sarah laughed.

Alex sat on the edge of the bed and threw his arms around the frail woman. The pair held each other tightly with joy and relief.

"There is just one thing though," Alex said as the pair released each other and sat gazing at each other.

"Yes?" Lady Sarah said with a slight frown.

"Can we keep our engagement a secret until the brigadier comes home again?" Mr Hunter asked.

"What if the baby is born before that?" Lady Sarah asked.

"I will marry you before it is born," Alex promised.

"Very well, I agree," Lady Sarah said decisively.

The pair sat talking for a few hours, laughing and enjoying the presence of the other for the first time in weeks.

"I should go down and see how the doctor is," Alex said finally, "his sister was taken by the witch."

"Oh no, I will come too," Lady Sarah said as she tried to climb out of bed, but Alex stopped her.

"You need to rest, please, for me," Mr Hunter begged, and Sarah begrudgingly returned to her book.

Reading was something that Lady Sarah enjoyed, but when she was confined to a single room, it was difficult to enjoy anything. People came to see her throughout the day, but they could all leave again and she could not, making any visit bittersweet.

After Mr Hunter had left, Lady Sarah did not expect any more visitors until dinner was ready and Mrs Bosworth would bring her evening meal to be eaten in bed before she would be given a sleeping draught to help her rest comfortably through the night.

But only half an hour after Alex had left, there was another knock at her door.

"Enter," Lady Sarah said and put her book down as Constable Evans came into her room. The constable had a very severe expression on his face as he walked across the room and looked out of the window at the grounds of the Grangeback Estate.

"Lady Sarah, you need to stay away from the woods until we have found this witch," Arwyn said without greeting her or waiting for her to greet him.

"Why? What's going on?" Sarah asked with a frown.

"The witch is only taking a specific group of people. A

man and woman in a relationship that our society disapproves of that also involves a child," Arwyn replied as he turned to look at her with a grim look on his face.

"You know?" Lady Sarah sighed and looked down at her blankets.

"Yes, and though I am happy for you both, it leaves you in great danger. Promise me that you will not go into the woods," Constable Evans said fiercely.

"I promise," Lady Sarah lied.

Chapter 17

If there was anything that was certain to have Lady Sarah Montgomery Baird, Watson-Wentworth stirring from her bed, it was a mystery that had to be solved.

The moment Constable Evans had told her to avoid the woods, Lady Sarah knew it was the one place she had to go. Neil had spent the night at Grangeback and seemed to have recovered from the shock of seeing his father and brother taken by the witch, and though the lady did not want to traumatise the boy any further, she needed to know what he had seen.

Mrs Bosworth had protested, but Lady Sarah had firmly refused to be denied. The two walked down towards the lake not long after breakfast with Pattinson following the pair.

"I want to look at every place that people have vanished from, and you need to tell me everything you can remember," Lady Sarah said gently to the boy as they walked.

"We were playing hide and seek. I was hiding in the tree. Father was kissing Miss Hales. Brendan was looking for me in the bushes. Then all of a sudden fog appeared. It was really strange. Then the witch came out of the fog and took all of them, but she left their clothes behind," Neil said, his lip quivering, at the memory.

"Well done," Lady Sarah said as she smiled at the boy and Pattinson licked the boy's hand. Neil grinned and threw his arms around the neck of the dog and buried his face in the thick fur of the Akita.

Alex had not come with them to search the forest that morning as he had other business to take care of. He walked with Sarah and Neil partway into the woods but then left to call on Reverend Percy Butterfield with Mr Frederick Anson. Alex and the dean of Chester had spent a few hours the night before discussing the best thing to do for Stickleback Hollow and the festival.

After a few minutes of discussion with the reverend, all three men were agreed that the festival should be postponed until the witch had been caught.

"Then we should go talk to Constable Evans and tell him what has been decided," Mr Hunter said.

The three men set off to find the constable. They knew that he wouldn't be at the police house, so decided to make a circuit around the village until they found him.

It took them nearly an hour to find Arwyn, but it didn't take them long to convince the constable that the festival needed to be postponed.

"How is Lady Sarah this morning? Feeling any better?" Constable Evans asked Mr Hunter after the decision had been made.

"Very well, she and young Neil went down to the woods together. She needed some fresh air," Alex replied with a smile.

"She promised to stay away from the woods," Arwyn said, shaking his head and set off towards the lake at a run.

"Where are you going?" Alex shouted after the constable.

"To fetch the lady home," the constable yelled back. Alex looked at the reverend and dean. None of them understood why her ladyship shouldn't be in the woods after being cooped up in the manor for so long.

"We should discuss how the festival is to be postponed and what effect it will have on those that have come a long way to be here," the reverend said.

"An excellent plan. A table at Wilson's Inn should suffice," the dean grinned and the hunter followed the two men of the cloth to the inn.

The inn was not especially quiet, but there were several free tables that the men could choose from. Mrs Cooper had taken up residence in the bar, drinking away the little money she had and ranting about how Miss Wessex was the witch.

Besides this disturbance, there was nothing that would stop the three men from talking. They settled down, and Wilson brought over a round of drinks for them.

There was a lot to talk about, and no one interrupted their discussions. Many people had heard rumours about the witch, but as the disappearances had been so isolated, only Neil had seen the witch and most had dismissed it as part of the festivities.

The men were halfway through their second round of drinks when the door to the inn opened, and Constables Cantello and McIntyre walked in.

"Mr Hunter, we're sorry to interrupt, but we need your help," Constable McIntyre said as he and Constable Cantello stood either side of the groundskeeper.

"What is it?" Alex asked as he looked between the two men with curiosity.

"Come with us, we'll speak outside," Constable

Cantello replied.

"If you'll excuse us, gentlemen," Alex said, looking confused, but he did as the two constables asked. When they were outside, the two constables kept walking until they reached the stables. It was the quietest part of the village during the festival and the safest place to talk without being overheard.

"What is going on?" Mr Hunter asked with frustration.

"Have you seen Constable Owens?" Constable Cantello asked.

"No, why?" Alex frowned.

"The disappearances of a man, woman and child, they've been happening up and down the country, and all of them in places where Constable Owens happens to have been posted. Someone is always arrested and hanged for murder, but it's too much of a coincidence for my liking," Constable McIntyre explained.

"Especially as some of the disappearances have gone hand-in-hand with a rumour about a witch in the area," Constable Cantello added.

"And a man that no one has been taking any notice of since he arrived," Alex mused, "Arwyn has gone down to the lake to find Lady Sarah and Neil Taylor, I'll find them and tell them about Constable Owens. If he is anywhere in the area, he should be on the top of the edge. There's an altar up there that someone has built recently," Mr Hunter said and set off at a run towards the woods.

Chapter 18

Constable Evans had been wandering through the trees for some time. He was not a good tracker and wished that he asked Mr Hunter to come with him to find the lady and the boy.

The constable was ready to turn back to the village to see if the pair had gone back, having searched the woods, but something caught his eye.

Mist was creeping its way through the trees; long fingers that twisted around the roots and trunks and rank between the leaves of the bushes and flowers. Arwyn had a sinking feeling in his chest as he watched the fog building in front of them. He heard screaming not far away and started to run.

He ran towards the scream, hoping it didn't belong to Lady Sarah. As the constable ran, the fog was thicker about his feet. He kept searching, his eyes scanning the trees for any sign of the boy and the lady. Then he saw the pair, Neil was running ahead of Lady Sarah, the young boy able to scramble through the trees and bushes more ably than the pregnant lady.

"Arwyn, run, get out of here!" Lady Sarah gasped as she tried to keep up the pace. Her eyes were wide with fright, and her skin had blanched.

Constable Evans kept running towards Lady Sarah despite her warnings, but then he saw something looming out of the fog that caused him to stop and stare with abject horror.

Out of the mist, the shape of a woman was emerging. She had wild hair that billowed out behind her and disappeared into the fog. Her body was covered in rags that looked as though they had been pulled at by wild animals. Her hands were reaching out, trying to reach out for those she was pursuing.

Arwyn shook his head with disbelief.

"Run!" Sarah screamed. The policeman did as he was told and ran, Neil was much further ahead of the two adults and almost clear of the fog. Arwyn ran as fast as he could, trying not to stumble over roots and bushes. But Lady Sarah was not so lucky.

She risked a glance back over her shoulder to see where the witch was, and as she took her eyes from her path, she caught her foot on a tree root.

She fell hard, the impact with the ground winding her a moment too long. The witch squealed with glee as the fog enveloped the fallen lady.

"Sarah!" Constable Evans called out. He had cleared the fog and looked round to see where the lady was. The witch stood over where the lady had fallen, cackling, and with no warning at all, the witch vanished.

The fog began to clear, and Lady Sarah had gone.

Neil began to cry, and Arwyn stood staring around the forest, unable to believe what he had just seen.

The policeman thought carefully for a minute about what he had to do. He grabbed Neil by the shoulders and knelt in front of him.

"The witch is gone. She can't hurt you. You have to run back to Grangeback. Don't stop. Go straight to the house and find the doctor. Tell him to come to Wilson's Inn as fast as he can. Tell him that Constable Evans sent you. If he won't come, tell him that it's about the baby. Do you understand?" Arwyn said, and Neil stopped crying. He sniffed and nodded. Constable Evans released his shoulders, and the boy was off like a shot. He raced off through the trees towards the village, nearly knocking down Mr Hunter as the two passed on the narrow path.

"Arwyn?" Alex called out as he spotted the constable through the trees.

"Alex, thank God. She took her, I couldn't stop it," Constable Evans shook his head helplessly.

"What are you talk about?" Alex frowned at his friend.

"The witch, she took Lady Sarah. She fell in the fog and then she was gone," Arwyn said, shaking his head. Mr Hunter stared at the constable for a moment, unsure of how to respond.

"It's Owens, he's the one behind it all. There's an altar and pentagram that someone has built on the top of the Edge. Edryd and I found it, but the witch took Miss Hales, Mr Taylor and his son before we could do anything," Alex said sadly.

"Then that must be where they are, the people that are taken," Arwyn said suddenly, hope in his voice.

"Where?" Alex asked.

"In the mine. No one would go in there to look for people that a witch kidnapped, but the legend -" Constable Evans began.

"Says there is a sleeping army beneath the Edge and the

mine tunnels riddle the hillside so there are plenty of places to hide people that would never be found," Mr Hunter finished the thought.

The two men took off on foot, moving as fast as they could. Pattinson had not been with Lady Sarah or Mr Hunter that morning. Instead, Derwyn had taken him to try and protect Miss DeVille whilst they were walking in the woods.

As Mr Hunter and Constable Evans ran through the trees, Pattinson knew that his master was coming. With a happy bark, the dog ran from Derwyn's side until he came across Alex and Arwyn, and fell into step beside them.

"Glad to have you here, boy," Mr Hunter said warmly as he dog barked.

They ran until their lungs hurt and then pushed on. When the ground under their feet began to slope upwards, they slowed their pace, and it wasn't long until they came across Constables McIntyre and Cantello moving slowly up the hill.

"It's a lot steeper than it looks," Constable Cantello smiled when he saw the two men approaching.

"Thought we could use some help?" Constable McIntyre asked as he looked between the two men.

"The witch took Lady Sarah. I saw it happen," Constable Evans said flatly.

"Then we should hurry," Constable Cantello replied and began to move up the Edge with more purpose than before.

As the men approached the top of the huge hill, Pattinson began to growl. All of his fur stood on end, and his teeth were barred.

"Easy boy," Alex said, placing his hand on the dog's neck to stop him charging off, "Wait here," he said to the others and slowly edged forward until he could see the site of the pentagram and altar.

Constable Owens was stood in front of the altar with a large book open. He was chanting with his arms raised and before him was a spectral form in the fog. Alex frowned as the form seemed to change between different women's faces as the mist moved in the wind.

He crept back down to where the others waited, carefully to keep hold of Pattinson as he moved.

"There is just Owens and the witch up there," Mr Hunter said.

"Then we rush in and take him by surprise," Constable

Evans shrugged.

"Into the valley of death," Constable McIntyre sighed.

They dared not wait too long, so the four men rose to their feet and charged forwards. With the hand taken from his neck, Pattinson barrelled in first, the dog snapping and growling. He charged, not at Constable Owens, but at the witch. He ran at full speed, leapt into the air and tried to snap at the apparition. Instead, his teeth met nothing, and he fell straight through the witch, landing at first on the altar, but his momentum meant that he only knocked everything off it. He kept going and landed against Constable Owens, knocking the man from his feet.

As the altar was cleared and Constable Owens flattened, the witch that had been facing him disappeared.

"Good boy, Pattinson!" Constable McIntyre laughed as he stopped running and took Constable Owens by the arm.

"You better come with us," Constable Cantello said to the junior policeman with a glint of malice in his eyes.

Constable Evans and Mr Hunter did not stop to watch the policemen arrest Constable Owens; instead, they pulled open the gate over the mine entrance and began to slowly move inside.

"This is hopeless without torches," Arwyn said after a few moments.

"Then go back and get them. Wilson has some horses you can borrow coming back," Alex said as he sat down in the mine and stared down the dark shaft.

"I sent for Doctor Hales, he should be at the inn, I'll bring him too. Just in case," Arwyn said and left the hunter sitting in the mine.

Pattinson padded into the darkness, his nose in the air. He didn't need the light that humans did, and so he walked off into the dark without his master, following his nose.

Alex didn't know how long it was that he sat waiting in the dark, but the most terrible thoughts ran through his mind and tortured him as he waited.

By the time Constable Evans returned, Alex looked as though he had aged ten years, all through worry. Arwyn was not alone as he returned. With him had come the doctor and Edryd as well as Thomas, Edward, Richard, Gordon and some of the other gentlemen that were all staying at Grangeback.

They had torches, and the doctor had a supply of blankets, water and laudanum.

"The grocer, butcher and blacksmith are all bringing

carts up from the village, just in case," the doctor said as he greeted Alex.

"What are you doing here?" Alex asked as Richard handed him a torch.

"Too many women have been disappearing. I won't have you moping because we couldn't find your woman. Gordon's moping is bad enough," Richard replied as he slapped his friend's back.

The tunnels that had formed the mine ran for miles, and it would have taken days for the men to search all of them. Pattinson, on the other hand, knew exactly where to go. He had left Alex sitting alone in the dark, but now that he could hear men moving down the tunnels towards him, the dog padded his way back to show the men where to go.

None of the men were prepared for the sight that greeted them. The first sight was the dead boy of Miss Elizabeth Wessex. In her hand, she clutched a piece of paper, but there was no way to take it out of her hand in the cramped conditions of the mineshaft.

Beside Miss Wessex were the bodies of those that had vanished from the lake. Their clothes were stained with water and their faces fixed with fear. But though the bodies were grotesque to look upon, it was nothing compared to how they smelled.

Then they came across Miss Jessica Hales. The woman looked more like a skeleton than a woman. Doctor Hales feared her dead until she slowly moved her head, opened her eyes and said,

"Where have you been? I've been waiting here for hours."

The doctor began to cry with relief and carefully picked up his sister and carried her out of the mine, Richard walking beside him to light the way.

Mr Taylor and his son were the next to be found, though aside from being dirty, hungry, in dire need of water, a hot bath, and a change of clothes, they were unharmed.

Last to be found was Lady Sarah. The moment that the light from the torches fell upon her, Mr Hunter was by her side.

"What kind of madness drove him to this?" Gordon asked as he and Edryd walked out of the mine together.

Thomas and Edward carried the body of Miss Wessex, the other three bodies were carried by the guests of Lady Sarah. Arwyn helped Mr Taylor and Brendan to leave, whilst

Alex carried his bride-to-be.

"Was it madness, or was it magic? A desire to control dark powers by sacrificing human lives?" Edryd shuddered.

"Or was it just a man that was mad and played tricks on everyone because he desired to kill. After all, how many people saw a witch in the fog because they had been told there was one?" Gordon replied.

"Whatever his reasons, he cannot harm anyone else now," Edryd replied.

"What will happen to him?" Gordon asked.

"I suspect he'll be hanged. It won't be a long trial, not when Miss Wessex was one of his victims. No, he'll be swiftly executed," Edryd said firmly.

"I suppose there is now nothing to stop the festival from continuing," Gordon said with a slight smile.

"Still have your eyes on that prize?" Edryd asked.

"We'll get to the centre of the maze first," Gordon said positively.

As they stepped out into the dim light of the fading afternoon, Arwyn was surprised to see Constable McGill was waiting for him.

"Has he said anything?" Arwyn asked.

"Oh, plenty. He was punishing sinners by summoning dark powers. Nothing sinful in that as far as he was concerned. But it was the women he wanted to hurt. He claimed that they were the sinners causing the men around them to sin and those that had been corrupted had to be destroyed along with those that corrupted them," Constable McGill replied with disgust.

"Has the reverend been to see him yet?" Arwyn asked.

"No, but I am sure he'll have a verse or two for the boy when he does. We'll have him in Chester by tonight. Leaves you very short-handed though," Constable McGill said with a slight smile.

"Just the way I like it then," Arwyn sighed.

Chapter 19

The festival was not postponed. As the source of the disappearances had been stopped, there was no need to end the frivolities. Stickleback Hollow returned to a state of some calm and the evening entertainments were restored.

Richard and Gordon Hales were the first to reach the centre of the maze and found a trophy filled with fresh fruits and vegetables from the harvest was the prize. The pair could not split the cup, so they gave it to their father to display with their other trophies.

Mr Hunter was relieved to have Lady Sarah safe at home again and vowed that he would never let her out of his sight again. That night, after the rest of the household was asleep, the hunter crept through the house to sleep beside his fiancée and the future mother of his child.

He felt a great sense of peace as he held the woman in his arms, but it was a peace that was short-lived. It was the early hours of the morning when Lady Sarah began to shake and scream with pain. Mr Hunter leapt from his bed and raced to rouse the doctor from his. The house was in uproar as the screaming of the young lady woke the whole house.

"I must get her to the hospital, go get the carriage at once," the doctor ordered when he saw the state that Lady Sarah was in.

Mr Hunter rushed down the stairs to help the stable boys prepare the carriage.

"What's wrong with her?" Alex demanded as the doctor carried Sarah from the house and placed her in the carriage.

"Get inside and keep her calm," the doctor said in reply.

"Tell me what is going on," Alex shouted.

"It's the baby. She is losing the baby, and if we are not quick, we will lose her too," the doctor said in a low voice.

Mr Hunter was stunned by the thought that little over a day after he had asked the young lady to marry him, he might lose her and the baby. He climbed into the carriage and held her tightly in his arms as the doctor cracked the whip and the carriage lurched forwards.

The baby was lost, but by some miracle, Lady Sarah survived. She was as pale as the witch in the woods had been, and ordered to remain in bed under the strict care of Doctor Hales.

Mr Hunter and Lady Sarah both grieved for the loss of their child, but they still had each other. Pattinson had taken to lying beside Lady Sarah on the bed and refused to move, save for meals and his occasional trips to the flower beds.

"It's a sad business," Edryd said as he sat in the brigadier's study with Doctor Hales. The two men had shut themselves away from the rest of the guests in the house, especially as Derwyn had brought Miss DeVille with him to enjoy the evening festivities.

"Indeed it is," the doctor agreed as he sipped his brandy.

"What has been said to the other guests?" Edryd asked.

"The shock of being kidnapped gave her nightmares that manifested in physical pain, a reaction to a severe trauma, but she is recovering and simply needs time to let her mind and body recover fully," Jack said with a wry smile.

"Such an evil thing to happen to the pair of them though, the witch had the last blood in the end it seems," Edryd said shaking his head.

"I wouldn't be so quick to jump to superstition as an

explanation," the doctor said with a slight frown.

"Then what do you think it was?" Edryd asked as he emptied his glass.

"Stress, the stress of the whole ordeal was too much for her already weakened body and the baby could not survive," Jack shrugged as though the reason was so simple it did not need to be explained.

Edryd sat back and began to laugh, but his laughter was interrupted by the door of the study being flung open. In the doorway stood   Lee and Stanley Baker, both looking breathless and terrified.

"What is wrong with you two now?" the doctor asked irritably.

"The witch, sir. We saw her," Lee stammered.

"What? Where?" Edryd asked.

"Just outside on the lawns. She was looking up at Lady Sarah's room," Stanley stuttered.

Edryd and Jack both moved to look out of the study windows, but all the pair could see was the tiniest wisp of fog fading into the night.

~*~*~

Love the book? Need to know what's next in Stickleback Hollow?

Bed bound in hospital, a mystery is out of reach, but when the doctor disappears too. She puts her life on line to find out what is going on. Can Lady Sarah find the doctor in time, or has it finally run out for both of them.

Get ***The Advent of Stickleback Hollow*** now!

~*~*~

Looking for more than just books? You can get the latest releases from me, signed paperbacks and hardbacks, mugs, t-shirts, journals and much more from my Read Round the Clock

Shopify store.

~*~*~

Love the Mysteries of Stickleback Hollow? Not caught up with the rest of the series, then jump back to _A Thief in Stickleback Hollow_, Book 1 in the Mysteries of Stickleback Hollow and see how it all began.

~*~*~

Want to help a reader out? Review are crucial when it comes to helping readers choose their next book and you can help them by leaving just a few sentences about this book as a review. It doesn't have to be anything fancy, just what you liked about the book and who you think might like to read it.

If you don't have time to leave a review or don't feel confident writing one, recommending a book to your family, friends and co-workers can help them choose their next book, so feel free to spread the word.

Historical Note

Gossip and reputation were something that could destroy a woman in Victorian society very quickly, something that the New Poor Law made worse in 1834. It had something called The Bastardy Clause that enabled men to walk away from their responsibilities without any worry and leave the mother to be shamed and raise the child. The New Poor Law meant that rather than restoring virtue, it gave rise to something very dark and even murderous – baby farming. The Poor Law of 1733 was actually far more socially advanced than it's replacement. Under it, fathers of illegitimate children had to pay maintenance in order to support the child, and if he didn't, the mother could have him put in prison until he started paying up. Whilst the father was in prison, the mother was even paid out of local public funds, which the father had to later repay. Local authorities, however, didn't like having to pay out, so they often tried to make the fathers marry the mothers.

When the New Poor Law came into effect, it meant that if a mother couldn't support her children, then she and her children would have to go to a workhouse and the father didn't have to do a damn thing. This led to many villainising the mothers of illegitimate children with the women denounced as part of "the lazy, worthless, and ignominious class who pursue their self-gratification at the expense of their earnings of the industrious part of the community." Women were the guilty ones and men were just the innocent bystanders in it all. Yet, not everyone agreed with the law and the Lord Chancellor's view that women were to blame. They instead held that women were the victims and men were to blame as seducers and should not be able to walk away. That by allowing the father to walk away, he was free to create as many bastards as he pleased without any consequence to himself – something that would only increase the number of illegitimate children, not decrease it as the law was attempting to do.

Elizabeth Gaskell wrote a book entitled *Ruth,* a book that deals with unwed mother's and their children, and unlike other books dealing with illegitimacy, actually tried to highlight how the mothers and children were victimised and that society was, in fact, the cause of the illegitimacy. The novel was met with great hostility, and many middle-class girls were told that it was forbidden and unsuitable reading material.   Orphanages began to refuse to take illegitimate children, claiming there were not lawfully begotten orphans. The idea that illegitimate children were more sinful than other children was also circulated, the thinking being that the illegitimate children would inherit all the sinful behaviours of their mothers.

In 1842, the Poor Law Commissioner even issued an order that mothers of illegitimate children and their children were to be kept out of workhouses so they wouldn't cause other women and girls of good character in the workhouses to sin. Girls who became pregnant when unwed were often ostracised from their homes, forced to leave in disgrace and moved to somewhere new and start a new life. This is where the baby farming came in. If you don't know what baby farming is, it's what it sounds like. People were paid to take illegitimate children from unwed mothers on the understanding that they would be raised properly by those that were being paid. The wealthy sometimes paid villages to raise their children through the difficult baby years until they were toddlers and then return them to their wealthy families (this happened to Jane Austen and her siblings). There was no real foster and adoption structure within British Law, so both fell under baby farming.

Those who took in the child were paid a lump sum for taking in the child, but not given regular payments to help with the cost of raising a baby. This meant it was more profitable for those baby farming to take in the child and then for it to die as they got to keep the money. You may already see where this is headed, many people adopted numerous children and then left them to die of neglect, whilst others just murdered the children put into their care. Fortunately, the law did catch on to this, and several of those who did this were tried for murder, criminal neglect and manslaughter, and hanged as a result. Margaret Waters is one of the more famous cases and was executed in 1870. The last baby farmer to be executed in Britain was Rhoda Willis, who was executed in 1907 in Wales.

It wasn't until 1870 that any real investigation was done into baby farming. It was an undercover investigation that seems to have been sparked by an event in 1865 that I will come to later. The 1870 investigation was reported in a letter to the Times and concluded that "children are murdered in scores by these women, that adoption is only a fine phrase for slow or sudden death."

It wasn't until 1872 that Parliament passed the Infant Life Protection Act.   Another act was passed in 1897 that controlled the registration of women who were responsible for more than one infant under the age of five for more than 48 hours. The Children's Act of 1908 meant that no child could be kept in a home that was unfit or overcrowded. More legislation was passed over the following 70 years that meant that foster care and placed adoption came under the regulation and protection of the state.

Baby farmers often advertised their services in local newspapers that would read as:

"NURSE CHILD WANTED, OR TO ADOPT -- The Advertiser, a Widow with a little family of her own, and moderate allowance from her late husband's friends, would be glad to accept the charge of a young child. Age no object. If sickly would receive a parent's care. Terms, Fifteen Shillings a month; or would adopt entirely if under two months for the small sum of Twelve pounds."

Mothers who went to baby farmers knew that they would never see their children again, but had no other choice as unwed mothers of illegitimate children could often not find work, could not receive support from the local authorities and had a child to support. Though twelve pounds was a lot of money back then, baby farmers only cared about how much money they could get for the child. Most of the time, the fathers of the babies were forced to pay the baby farmers. Paying a sum like twelve pounds was often preferable to scandal, and it meant that they could dispose of their shame and the child was effectively condemned to death.

The lack of law until 1872 showed one thing, that illegitimate children were less important than animals, as there were strict laws against mistreating animals and if you kept cows, there were even strict licensing laws. But there was no licensing involved for baby farmers. There are many horror stories about baby farming, and most are so horrific to modern sensibilities that I will not scar you with the details, though there is one story that caused baby farming to suddenly become an international concern in 1865. The story of baby farmer, Charlotte Winsor. On 15th February 1865, the body of a boy was found wrapped in a newspaper lying beside the road in Torquay. The body was that of Mary Jane Harris' four-month-old son that had been farmed out to Charlotte Winsor. Mrs Winsor was paid 3 shillings a week to take care of the child and put pressure on Miss Harris to agree to have the child disposed of. Miss Harris resisted at first, but as the financial pressure of paying 3 shillings a week became too much, she stood by and watched Charlotte Winsor smother her infant son and wrap it in a newspaper. It was later dumped by the side of the road – funerals were too expensive for the likes of him. It was discovered during her trial that Charlotte Winsor had a lively business in baby farming. Though there was a huge amount of public pressure at the time for reform, this soon disappeared when Winsor was sent to prison. It wasn't until the horrors of Mrs Waters in 1870 that baby farming final received the attention it needed. In short, Mrs Waters drugged and starved 16 infants to death in just a few weeks, wrapped their bodies in newspapers and dumped them on deserted streets. When she was arrested, there were nine children in her home that were taken to a workhouse. Most of them died not long after from thrush and fluid on the brain.

There are many, many baby farming horror stories that could be told, and even more that have permeated into fiction from the time. It is therefore understandable that a desperate mother would leave her twin infant sons on the doorstep of a good woman instead of sending them to their deaths through baby farming. Though Stanley and Lee Baker will not know their good fortune until much later in life, there are so many poor children that were murdered for nothing more than being born to mothers that had no support and were ostracised by a society consumed with blaming one individual for something it takes two to do – and an act in which there was sometimes only one willing participant.

China patterns, something a little more cheery. China patterns were extremely varied in the Victorian age and something that I wanted to highlight with Mr Claydon's collection of mismatched china. As an explorer, I felt it would be very possible that his china was routinely broken as he moved about so that he was only left with items that didn't match and rather whimsically decided to lean into mismatching.

Plum cake was a popular treat as many of the cakes that are popular today had yet to come into existence or some into fashion. The plum cake was an easy dish to make and contained the following ingredients: - raisins, currants, dried apricots, cherries, lemon rind, orange rind, almonds, sherry, butter, brown sugar, treacle, cinnamon, nutmeg, ginger, cloves, flour, eggs and apricot wine.

Chewing nosily is a reference to me. According to my partner, Matt, when I am eating something I love, and it is just the two of us, I am an incredibly noisy eater. Not chewing noises but gulping and generally enjoying my food (and drink) so much so, he tells me that I often sound out of breath when I am done.

Poachers have been a problem for centuries, and it is a problem that persists to this day, though it is now more commonly associated with the slaughter of endangered species. Originally, in Britain, poaching was the illegal hunting of animals by those that were too poor to afford meat. Those that were poor often killed deer and other wild animals that lived on estates and private land and thus belonged to the nobility.

Poaching was a hanging offence after it was established as a crime in William the Conqueror's forest law that made the hunting of animals in forests the province of nobles only, not the common man – something that was not very well received by the population of William's new country. Though it was not well received, it was very well enforced and land rights as well as the Night Poaching Act 1828 and Game Act of 1831 secured the rights of landowners to the animals on their property. This did not stop people from poaching though. Poachers would create traps in order to secure animals without the aid of guns that could be heard and clearly identified. An animal falling into a pit or getting caught in a snare were much more subtle ways of poaching. However, poachers were as much prey as the animals they hunted. Landowners would lay man traps on their land to catch poachers (what many would now consider a bear trap). It had metal jaws that could be forced apart and were held open by a small catch. A plate in the centre was the trigger, and the slightest amount of pressure on the plate would cause the jaws to slam closed. The man trap was outlawed in 1826, but in 1830 a law was passed that enabled landowners to apply for a licence to use them.   Poachers were also chased down by men with dogs and guns.

The trap that Jamie Williamson's leg was caught in was a Gin Trap (or leghold trap) that have been illegal in the UK since 1958. There are lots of different styles of gin traps, and none of them are friendly-looking pieces of equipment. If you want to see some example of gin traps, https://www.vintagetraps.co.uk/product-category/all-products/vintage-traps/gin-traps/ has a varied selection and shows a range of styles and different sized traps to give you an idea of what caused the poor boy so much pain.

Parish Councils meetings is a term that you might be familiar with, but these were not around in the 1830s; instead, there were Church Vestry meetings. Communication was very poor, and villages were often overseen by the Lord of the Manor. In 1600 AD, the church took a more active role in local governance, and Church Vestry meetings were established as was the responsibility of the church to levy the poor-rate (the first local taxes). Everyone and anyone was allowed to come to Church Vestry Meetings, but like modern Parish Councils, the work was taken on by a few individuals rather than the community as a whole. In the 1800s, the Poor Law was amended, and poor relief was moved into the hands of Poor Law Unions, which later became District Councils. The Lord of the Manor and the reverend were still village leaders, people wanted more of a say in the management of local affairs. In 1894, the Local Government Act became law, despite considerable opposition, and Parish Councils were formed as we know them now. The Parish Councils are responsible for civil matters, and church matters are in the hands of the Parochial Church Council (something that many people often get confused about).

The teacup was not brought to Europe until the 17th century, They were exports from Japan and China and were small ceramic bowls without handles. It wasn't until 1707 when Johann Friedrich Bottger got hold of the teacup that the handle was introduced. At the turn of the century (1799 to 1800) the deeper canns with a handle and more cylindrical form became the fashion rather than the traditional bowl-shaped teacups, and they had persisted to this day. High-end teacups are general made of fine white porcelain and are said to provide a better taste than simply having tea in a mug.

Praise my soul, the King of heaven is a hymn that was written much earlier than it was put to music. The lyrics are something that the Reverend Percy Butterfield could have well-read, but there would have been no official score to the song until 1868. It was written by Henry Francis Lyte in 1834, and John Goss composed Lauda Anima in 1868 to accompany the lyrics.

As well as it being a rather stirring hymn, it is also my family hymn, and therefore it was something I had to include at some point in these stories.

Frederick Anson replaced George Davys as the dean of Chester when Davys was made the Bishop of Peterborough. Frederick Anson was married to Mary Anne Levett and remained as the dean of Chester from 1839 until his death in 1867, so expect to see more of him in the future. The Anson family is one of the British aristocratic families and is currently headed by the 6th Earl of Lichfield. The house motto is "Never despairing", and it was found 249 years ago in 1770. Frederick Anson was the son of George Anson, the British politician and father of Frederick Anson who was named Canon of Windsor by Queen Victoria in 1844. His other son, George, was a British politician and courtier. He served as private secretary to Prince Albert as well as holding the titles of Keeper of Her Majesty's Privy Purse, Treasurer of the Household to HRH Prince Albert, and Treasurer and Cofferer of the Household of HRH the Prince of Wales. He also served as a member of the Council of the Duchy of Lancaster and a member of the Prince of Wales's Council for the Duchy of Cornwall.

Cockney Rhyming Slang wasn't invented until a little later in the Victorian period than this book is set, and you may be wondering what cockney rhyming slang has to do with any of the things that happen in this book. When Doctor Hales refers to Miss Jessica Hales as "skin", it's a reference to the cockney rhyming slang phrase "skin and blister" that means sister. Though it is unlikely that the doctor or anyone else in Stickleback Hollow would know a regional dialect code like cockney rhyming slang, it is something I have heard since I was a little girl as my aunt and mother refer to each other as "skin" in the most affectionate way, and I wanted to include it in this book.

Hedge Mazes originated in Renaissance Europe in the mid-16th century. They are outdoor mazes with walls made from tall vertical hedges that make it impossible to cut through unless there are gaps. The idea of hedges mazes grew out of knot gardens, and hundreds of mazes were made all across Europe between the 16th and 18th centuries. The oldest surviving hedge maze in Britain can be found at Hampton Court Palace. It is a trapezoid in shape making it distinctive, though the shape was dictated by the existing paths that ran beside it.

Originally they were designed not as labyrinths, but as walking paths and were lined with evergreen herbs and dwarf box. Hedges mazes as puzzles came to England during King William III's reign (who had the maze built at Hampton Court).

One of the most beautiful and confusing mazes to ever have been created was at the Palace of Versailles. It was built for Louis XIV in 1677 and featured 39 hydraulic sculpture groups that showed Aesop's fables. It was destroyed in 1778; however, diagrams and engravings of the Labyrinth de Versailles still exist so that the beauty of the maze can be appreciated still to some extent.

Hedge mazes can still be found all over the United Kingdom and are a rather fun way to spend an afternoon.

Though the Victorian Era is seen as one as a search for knowledge, industry and scientific fact, it was also the time when supernatural belief was at its height. I am not talking matters of religion, but rather the belief in ghost stories, hauntings, werewolves, transformations, witches, supernatural forces at work, dark energies and other phenomena. It is because of this that I wanted to write a story with a witch at the heart of it and leave it as unresolved as much as possible. Though we may now not see ghosts or witches riding at the head of mist trying to steal the souls of those lost in the woods, the mind can play tricks on you and many shadows cast by tree branches on dark stormy nights can look far more sinister than the branches that wave harmlessly outside your window during the day. The full extent of spiritualism in Victorian society I have yet to touch on, but for many at the time, witches flew across the skies at night and practised dark magic.

Into the valley of death is a reference to the poem by Alfred,

Lord Tennyson. I couldn't use it as a quote from the poem within the story as the poem wasn't written until 1854. The poem that I am referencing is the Charge of the Light Brigade, and if you haven't had the chance to read it before, it goes like this:

"Half a league half a league,
Half a league onward,
All in the valley of Death
Rode the six hundred:
'Forward, the Light Brigade!
Charge for the guns' he said:
Into the valley of Death
Rode the six hundred.

'Forward, the Light Brigade!'
Was there a man dismay'd ?
Not tho' the soldier knew
Someone had blunder'd:
Theirs not to make reply,
Theirs not to reason why,
Theirs but to do & die,

Into the valley of Death
Rode the six hundred.

Cannon to right of them,
Cannon to left of them,
Cannon in front of them
Volley'd & thunder'd;
Storm'd at with shot and shell,
Boldly they rode and well,
Into the jaws of Death,
Into the mouth of Hell
Rode the six hundred.

Flash'd all their sabres bare,
Flash'd as they turn'd in air
Sabring the gunners there,
Charging an army while

All the world wonder'd:
Plunged in the battery-smoke
Right thro' the line they broke;
Cossack & Russian

Reel'd from the sabre-stroke,
Shatter'd & sunder'd.
Then they rode back, but not
Not the six hundred.

Cannon to right of them,
Cannon to left of them,
Cannon behind them
Volley'd and thunder'd;
Storm'd at with shot and shell,
While horse & hero fell,
They that had fought so well
Came thro' the jaws of Death,
Back from the mouth of Hell,
All that was left of them,
Left of six hundred.

When can their glory fade?
O the wild charge they made!
All the world wonder'd.
Honour the charge they made!
Honour the Light Brigade,

Noble six hundred!"

Finally, there is one more thing to mention about this book. The plot for this book came to me in a dream and was fleshed out somewhat in order to create this story. Within the dream, I saw the witch appearing in the woods around water. A few years later, before I wrote this book, my uncle showed me a photograph he had taken in the woods, and it looked exactly like my dream. This has formed the background for this book's cover. The dream also gave rise to the whole of the Mysteries of Stickleback Hollow series, so though this is book number 8, it is where it all started.

About the Series
Mysteries abound

When her parents die from fever, Lady Sarah Montgomery Baird Watson-Wentworth has to leave India, a land she was born and raised in, and travel to England for the first time. Finding it almost impossible to adjust to London society, Sarah flees to the county of Cheshire and the country estate of Grangeback that borders the village of Stickleback Hollow. A place filled with oddballs, eccentrics and more suspicious characters than you can shake a stick at, Sarah feels more at home in the sleepy little village than she ever did in the big city, however, even sleepy little villages have mysteries that must be solved.

Set in Victorian England, the Mysteries of Stickleback Hollow follows the crime solving efforts of Constable Arwyn Evans, Mr. Alexander Hunter and Lady Sarah Montgomery Baird Watson-Wentworth. From theft to murder, supernatural occurrences and missing people, Stickleback Hollow is a magical place filled with oddballs, outcasts, rogues, eccentrics and ragamuffins.

Preview from the next book
The Advent of Stickleback Hollow

The front desk was vacant when Derwyn and Miss DeVille arrived at the hospital. Miss DeVille was somewhat relieved to find there was no nurse at the desk. Miss Beaumont had related the details of their visit in full to the pair, and Miss DeVille had been quite nervous at the prospect of having to argue her way into the hospital.

Miss Beaumont had also made sure that the pair knew how to get to Lady Sarah's room before they left Stickleback Hollow.

"If the doctor isn't there, then you will have to find your own way," Miss Beaumont had warned them, having no faith in Nurse Smith's ability to be helpful.

Derwyn was glad that Miss Beaumont had been so insistent with her instructions. The hospital corridors seemed like a maze to the Welshman, and he was certain that they would have become hopelessly lost in moments if they had not been given such detailed direction.

Miss DeVille was the first to reach the door to Lady Sarah's room and was surprised to find that it was open and that her ladyship already had visitors.

The two Baker boys were still talking animatedly to the lady, though Lady Sarah seemed to be close to falling asleep.

She was leaning back on her pillows, a contented smile on her face and her eyelids drooping.

"What's all this noise then?" Derwyn asked in a teasing voice as he stepped into the room. Miss DeVille hoovered outside the door, unsure if she should enter.

Lady Sarah turned her head, her smile broadening as she made to welcome her new visitors.

"Miss DeVille, Mr Evans, how kind of you to come," Lady Sarah said in a slightly quieter voice than she would have normally used.

"We thought that you might be in need of some company, but it seems that young Lee and Stanley have beaten us to it!" Derwyn said as he approached the two Baker boys and tousled their hair.

"We're sorry, your ladyship, we shouldn't have come.

We should go and let you rest," Miss DeVille said in a small voice from the doorway.

"Not at all, come and tell me your news," Lady Sarah gave Miss DeVille a small smile as she closed her eyes and listened to the Baker boys chattering to Derwyn, and Miss DeVille telling of all the things that she and Derwyn had done since Lady Sarah had come to the hospital.

Though Lady Sarah was exhausted from having so many people visit her all at once, it made her feel happier than she had felt in weeks.

The only thing that she was truly missing whilst she was restricted to the bed in the small hospital room was Mr Hunter. She did not ask about him or why he had not been to visit her. The truth about his absence was not something that she wanted to hear about from anyone for fear of how much it would hurt her.

His lack of presence, though painful, was bearable. Knowing that he simply no longer cared enough to visit her would be too much for her heart, already breaking from the loss of their child.

"Did you happen to see Doctor Hales as you came in?" Lady Sarah asked when Miss DeVille had finished sharing her news.

"No, in fact, we didn't see anyone at all between the hospital entrance and your room," Miss DeVille replied.

"How strange," Lady Sarah frowned.

"Why? Is there something you need from him?" Derwyn asked.

"He went to check on some records, but that was nearly two hours ago. I don't know where he could be. He brought Stanley and Lee with him, and I am not sure how they will get home again if he does not come back soon," Lady Sarah replied, looking with some concern at the two boys.

There was only so much time that two young boys could find sitting in a hospital entertaining. The excitement of seeing Lady Sarah and the arrival of Derwyn and Miss DeVille had been pleasant enough distractions, but it was clear that the Baker boys wanted to go home.

"We can take the boys back to the manor," Derwyn volunteered.

"Thank you, I do not want them to be stranded here for hours," Lady Sarah smiled with relief.

"Is there anything else that you need?" Miss DeVille asked as she rose to her feet and looked down at bed-bound lady.

"Could you ask Constable Evans and Mr Hunter to come this evening, please? There is something I need from them both," Lady Sarah said with a deep sigh.

She did not want to show any emotion when she mentioned Alex's name, but her voice wavered slightly. She wanted to see him desperately, but at the same time, she did not want to see him at all if he was only going to break her heart further.

Yet, if there was a mystery that lurked in the hospital, she needed the help of both Arwyn and Alex. The length of time that Doctor Hales had been gone made her nervous, and even more certain that there was something nefarious afoot.

"Constable Evans will certainly be willing to come, my lady. Derwyn, could you take the boys to the coach you borrowed from Grangeback? Ask the driver to prepare for our departure?" Miss DeVille said with a kind smile. Derwyn nodded and said farewell to Lady Sarah. Lee and Stanley waved goodbye and followed Derwyn from the hospital room.

Miss DeVille closed the door behind them. When she was sure that they were out of earshot, she sat back down beside Lady Sarah.

"What is wrong?" Lady Sarah asked with worry.

"Mr Hunter has turned to drink. I do not know how much Lee and Stanley know, but the idolise the man, and I do not want to speak ill of him in front of them. He is said to have locked himself in the brigadier's study at first, and now he is locked in the lodge. I do not know if anything that we say can make him unlock the door, but we will try," Miss DeVille said sadly.

"I see. Thank you," Lady Sarah said, biting her lip so that she would not cry.

"We will come and see you again. Take care," Miss DeVille said and left Lady Sarah alone in her room.

The moment that Miss DeVille had closed the door behind her, Lady Sarah burst into tears and sobbed into her hands. Things were far worse than she had feared.

Grab you copy now!

About the Author

I was born in Macclesfield, Cheshire, UK, and raised in the nearby town of Wilmslow. From an early age I discovered I had a flair and passion for writing.

I began writing at the age of 7 and was first published in 2010. I currently live with my partner, Matt, and our two cats in Christchurch, New Zealand.

As an avid horsewoman and gamer, I also have a passion for singing, dancing, the theatre, and my garden.

Facebook: https://www.facebook.com/AuthorC.S.Woolley

Instagram: https://www.instagram.com/thecswoolley

Website: http://.mightierthanthesworduk.com

Acknowledgements

Writing can be an extremely lonely profession at times, but thankfully I never have to go through any of the pressures alone. My wonderful Matthew has been a source of constant support to me during all of my writing endeavours since we first met. I couldn't ask for a more fitting partner to share my life or love with.

Writing is not something I stumbled into either, my mother, Helen, took me, and my sisters, to the library every weekend when we were young to get different books, and I always maxed out the number of books I could get. Not only did she encourage me to read, but to write as well. To say I have been writing stories and poetry since I was 7 is not an exaggeration and the development of my writing career is due in no small part to her.

My mother-in-law, Lesley, has also been a source of unflinching and unwavering support, something I could not do without.

To Laura and Sam, who have read and offered opinions, death threats and encouragement on my early drafts, you are true treasures. Amy, you too are worth your weight and more in gold for all your love and support.

It may seem that writers only function alone, but I am blessed to be part of an amazing community of authors whom I know that I have helped push me to even greater heights and success. So to Quinn Ward, Donna Higton, Charlene Perry, Scarlett Braden Moss, Bryan Cohen, Chez Churton, Eliza Green, John Beresford, Rich Cook, Robert Scanlon, Jen Lassalle, Cathy MacRae, Ariella Zoella, and Helen Blenkinsop, my dear friends, thank you.

And finally, to you, dear reader, without you there would be no books, no series, no career. I want to thank you for all the time that you spend reading my work, reviewing it, sharing it with your friends and family. Without you there would be nothing. Thank you from the bottom of my heart.

Until we meet again in my next book, thank you and adieu.